Nabarun Bhattacharya (1948–2014) was born into a family of writers, filmmakers, artists and academics—his father was playwright Bijan Bhattacharya; his mother, writer and activist Mahasweta Devi; his maternal grandfather, well-known *Kallol*-era writer, Manish Ghatak. Educated at Ballygunge Government School, Bhattacharya went on to study geology at Asutosh College and then English literature at City College. A journalist from 1973 to 1991 at a foreign news agency, he gave up that career in order to become a full-time writer. *Herbert* was published in 1992 and won the Bankim and Sahitya Akademi awards. Some of his best-known works are *Kangal Malshat* (2003), *Ei Mrityu Upotyoka Aamaar Desh Na* (2004) and *Phyataroor Bombachak* (2004). Novelist and short-story writer, he was also a prolific poet and, from 2003 until his death, editor of the *Bhashabandhan* journal.

Bhattacharya believed that every species has a right to exist without being at the mercy of humans, and one of his landmark novels, *Lubdhak* (2006), stems from this conviction. A devoted feeder of every stray dog and cat in the neighbourhood, he was also a keen watcher of insects, reptiles and other forms of life in his garden which he tended to for at least an hour every day. He also spent a lot of his time walking through the city, exploring its streets and lanes and bylanes, soaking in the conversations and experiences of his subjects.

His funeral procession in Calcutta was a strange one indeed—ministers and prominent cultural personalities marched alongside activists, former political prisoners and a sea of have-nots, a sea of his people. An offer of a state funeral was rejected by the family—it would have gone against the very grain of what he'd stood for, and written about, all his life.

NABARUN
BHATTACHARYA
Herbert

TRANSLATED BY
SUNANDINI BANERJEE

LONDON NEW YORK CALCUTTA

Seagull Books, 2019

Originally published in Bengali in 1994 as *Harbart*
by Deys Publishers, Calcutta
© Tathagatha Bhattacharya, 2014

English translation © Sunandini Banerjee, 2019

ISBN   978 0 8574 2 649 9

British Library Cataloguing-in-Publication Data
A catalogue record for this book is available from the British Library

Typeset by Seagull Books, Calcutta, India
Printed and bound by Hyam Enterprises, Calcutta, India

Herbert

One

No ties round my feet, no heart to my beat,
Eye-open nirvana, my soul waits, still.

—*Bijoychandra Majumdar*

·

'Let him sleep. He'll be all right if he sleeps.'

25th May. 1992. Borka had spoken those words on the way back from the office of 'Conversations with the Dead'—Herbert's room—spoken them deep into the night, late into the darkness, to the house in the lane, the road in the house, the house in the street, the house back home.

For Koton, Somnath, Koka, Daktar and Borka, the walk back home after the drinking that night . . . the memories of it are jumbled. Slime on the face of the moon. The streetlights surrounded by froth-foaming light-dust. Everything slippery with heat. And from the pits of their bellies, curdled chops and chana and whisky and rum and ice-water roaring up into their throats. Swarms of cockroaches seething out of the grilles over the gutter mouths and flying up into the streetlights' glow. Koka vomiting against the Dutta-house gates. Hot, sour and slimy vomit—Borka could still smell its acid reek. Daktar and Koton playing piss-cross games. A large cloud, like an oily sack, suddenly swallowing the moon. At the mouth of the cowmen's slums, a Corporation tap. A rag-clad mumble-mad woman sitting there, legs wide open, thrash-splashing water. Every now and then an owl letting out a screech and the skin-rotten street dogs rumb-grumbling in their dreams.

On the roof of the terrace room of Herbert Sarkar's house sat a Star-TV-signal-sucking satellite dish, gaping up at the night sky, hoping to swallow a falling star.

Daktar finished his pissing games and then looked at Koka, leaning against the Dutta-house gate. 'Drink. and puke. Don't drink, still puke. This is why I swear I don't like to drink with you lot. Screw the high! Screw the happiness! Racket and ructions—that's all you can do!'

'Herbert-da screwed!' Koton screamed, 'Herbert-da fucked!'

Koka was thinking that he'd never touch another drop in his life. But then he began to run, vomit-threads trailing from the corners of his mouth, because just then Somnath began to scream, loud enough to wake the street: 'Khororobi's coming! He's coming to feed you all fish!'

Drowned and dead a long time ago, he could still come, could Khororobi. Especially if Herbert-da called him.

That night, then, such had been the bandobast. A kick-ass-khatarnak googly. More often than not, such nights slid past in a haze, a booze glaze.

Sometimes, a dead breeze.

*

The large clock on the first-floor veranda struck. One. Chop chunks on sal-leaf plates, stripes of Gujarati-shop-chana gravy at the bottom of the clay pot—about eight cockroaches were relishing their dinner on the floor. A fat lizard slowly slid down the street-side wall, then crept up the leg of Herbert's bed and looked—was he asleep? Herbert was still. So still that the lizard crawled across his chest and then down his arm to his left hand, only to find it immersed in a bucket of blood-smelling cold water. Calculating the distance between arm and bucket rim, his green eyes shining in the dark, the lizard paused for a moment and then leapt. And then, just as he was thinking of sliding down and making his way over to the dinner of cockroaches, an extraordinary-amazing blue light filled the room. The lizard and the cockroaches were the only witnesses. On the outside wall, towards the alley, the closed window. And rubbing her face against its dirty-dusty glass, a fairy flapping her wings, trying to make her way into the room, trying to come close to Herbert. The blue heat of her blue face fogging up the glass, her blue tears washing it clean.

Herbert's eyes had been half-open then.

Someone had closed them later.

This night, then, such had been the bandobast.

Then, in the early hours of the morning, the ants had come. Ants know how to share, how not to fight and fisticuff. The black ants pick up the crumbs, the grain of dal stuck between the teeth and then picked out and flicked away. Dry food. Morsel and minuscule. The red ants and the large ants go straight for the nostrils, the phlegm, the eyes, the saliva at the corners of the mouth, the base of the tongue, the soft spots in the gums. And so on. Amid such a carnival of carnivores, it was but natural that a cacophony of crickets would be relegated to mere background music. For whether good days or bad, whether civilization or savagery, they have been singing the same song. Whether they are heard. Or not.

*

In the wall, a rusty iron hook. From it, hanging, on the inside, Herbert's curl-handled umbrella. Invisible to the naked eye for over it, like Dracula's cape, hung Herbert's Ulster overcoat. Near his head, in a shelf cut in the wall, lay two of his most important books:

(1) Mrinal Kanti Ghosh Bhaktibhushan's *Accounts of the Afterlife*. Revised and Enlarged, Second Edition. Price: 2 Rupees only. Upon closer examination, the book appears to begin at page 171. So the first thing you see is a photograph of Maharaj Bahadur Sir Jatindramohan Tagore KCSI. And beneath it, the information that on 14 January 1908, aged 77, he left this world for the great hereafter, and then the book began, thus—'[W]rote, "Mother, I have troubled you a lot, forgive me. I too have suffered but now I am finally resting in peace." Then, after writing many more such things, Shibchandra's wife burst out of her trance. She began to weep for her daughter . . .' Etc.

(2) Kalibar Bedantabagish's *Mysteries of the Afterlife*.

Herbert had found both these books in his grandfather Biharilal Sarkar's collection. Apart from *Mysteries of the Afterlife*, no book had been intact. No, one other book *had* been—Srigurupada Haldar's *A History of the Philosophy of Grammar, Volume One*. For obvious reasons, Herbert had never read that one. But he had read 'The Horribly Haunted Circus' in the bound but crumbling volume of *The Dance Hall* magazine. From that he had gathered the *out-knowledge* that the nicknames of the two actress sisters Suchinta and Sukumari had been Suchi and Bhudi, respectively; that Srimati Sushilasundari would *play* at

Professor Bose's Grand Circus; and that two other actresses, Hironmoyee and Mrinmoyee, alias Bhuti and Bhoma, resided at Beadon Street.

One could say that Herbert was attracted to them, by them, that he thought them familiars in a way that went beyond their ever meeting or living in the same time.

It was the dead of night. When, suddenly, the palace of Pithapur was set atremble by the frightened screams of the ladies and the confused shouting of the gentlemen. Who knows what ghastly ghostly creature had struck again—thinking thus, Gopal Duria and the rest of the stable hands ran towards the palace doors!

It would be no exaggeration to say that Herbert felt as though he had seen it all with his very own eyes.

Tired of flapping her wings against the windowpane, and afraid of the brightening sky, the fairy fled back to the shop.

The lizard and the cockroaches had, in any case, forgotten all about her.

Around midnight, when Herbert slashed the vein in his left hand, a fly trapped in his room, like a shark in the ocean, had smelt the blood. But it could not see, so it could do nothing. When drops of morning light began to seep into the room, it buzzed over to the blade fallen to the floor.

But the blood on it had dried black, long black, long ago.

Herbert's hand, its vein slashed, still hung still in the bucket of ice-cold water. His eyes, almost closed. His face, however, no longer as fair or as sharp-sharp as usual. But black. His mouth, a little open. His right hand, folded across his chest.

All that alcohol he'd sent for, it had been to dull the pain.

*

The one who'd written the letter, the photographer and the reporter, the college boys and girls—after they had all gone, Koton, Borka, Koka, Gyanobaan, Buddhi-maan, Somnath, Abhay, Khororobi's brother Jhaapi, Gobindo—all the boys rushed into the room and saw Herbert shiver-quivering. Gasping-clasping-unclasping, sweating. His shirt he'd thrown off. The table-fan swung from side to side, and with it swung Herbert, trying to catch the breeze. They stopped it swinging, made him sit on his bed, made him drink a glass of water. Sent for tea, special tea, until slowly, Herbert began to calm down. But the fear wouldn't leave his eyes. 'Thumping inside,' he kept saying, 'thump-thumping, thump-thumping inside...'

My god, what bandobast was this?

'Boss, relax. Calm down. Have some more tea?'

'No! I've had my last supper. Just beating. Only beating! Crawling, still beating. Flat on the floor, still beating. Punching slapping kicking beating . . .'

Herbert let out a heartrending wail, then began to tug at his hair. Kicked away the pillow. Leapt to his feet, looked at himself in the mirror on the wall shelf and then, still sobbing, suddenly stood straight and still. Smiled. 'Father-mother-dead khanki-kin, whoreson, wanted to earn your living by fucking with the ghosts? Couldn't bugger the living, so you had to bugger the dead? So, how does it feel now? To be pole-axed, rod-arsed? Deep in shit up to the roof of your mouth, how does it feel, Herbert? Her . . . bert, He . . . r . . . bert!'

Slapping his cheeks left and right, he begins to jump about the room. The boys grab him and drag him back to bed. His dhuti has fallen off. He is only in his *underwear*. He sits on the bed, his eyes closed, and sways, to and fro.

'I won't speak any more, I'm not speaking any more. Not any more, not a bubble more. Wait for as long as you want with the scale-scraping blade, won't see no sign of me. Peeyu kahaan, peeyu kahaan!'

'Guru, get a grip, please! Why don't you lie down?'

'No, let go. Stomach's turning. Churning.'

'Shit.'

'Maybe. Let me try.'

If Herbert needs a shit or a bath, he has to go down the street and round the house to the back door, the one used by the sweepers. That's where the servants were meant to go. As they glimpsed Herbert step out in his underwear, some kids on the street shouted 'Titbird, tit-bird!' Koton rushed out: 'One kick in your teeth, and you'll stay shut forever!' They ran away.

Back in the room, the boys wait for Herbert. They talk. 'Once he's had a shit, just see, boss will be fit again.'

The one named Daktar, he had a medicine shop. Studied only till Class Seven, but he knew a lot. 'I'm thinking something else. Often, before the heart chokes, one needs a shit, one wants to puke.'

'I've seen, when they're hanged, they shit them-selves.'

'Shut up! I'm talking of *heartchokes*, and you've gone off into hangings!'

'This is why his father named him Gyaanoban, fucking know-all.'

'Don't dare bring my father into this, Koka. I'll *pin* you I swear!'

They talk.

Outside, the blaze of the noonday sun is slowly enveloped by the magic-maya tendrils of early-evening light. A weak, golden glow. Suddenly they see Herbert, beautiful Herbert, standing there, the light like a halo round his head. His head is wet, his body, the hair on his chest. The hair on his head, plastered against his skull. His underwear, sopping-slopping wet. The water running off him in big fat drops, and Herbert laughing. Twirling into the room like a ballerina, he pulled his towel off the line and then, drying himself, said, 'Saw the tank overflowing with water. Thought I'd take a bath.'

'How you feeling now, boss?'

'Full of good feeling. Why don't we go out?'

'You won't drink tonight, boss?'

'Not drink tonight? Tonight's the gala-mela grand celebration! Tonight the booze will be extraordinary! Tonight we'll sky-fly sky-high.'

'Great! So you're mood's back, then!'

Herbert puts on a fresh dhuti. Talks as he ties it around him. Talks as he combs his hair. Then dons a hand-washed *full shirt*. Then opens the trunk. Then counts some money. Counts a lot of money. Counts so much he has to use finger-spit.

'Like we need to worry about moods. Know this: khanki-kin don't fuck about with all this mood-food. All we know is fun. How can I tell you what a time they're having, the katla fish on the babla tree. The bells are tinkling. The lights are flashing, flashing blue, flashing red, like a *dance party*. On the branches the gleam and the glitter of the big ones, the rui and the mirgel. And on the leaves, the little mourola, shining. Silver-sparkle. Sparkle-silver. No one can stop the bawaal-bedlam, I tell you! The shahebs beat us black and blue, day and night. Could they stop it? The shahebs got tired, then this lot arrived. Arrey baba, if English-spurting was all it needed to stop the bawaal, then . . .'

He tied a rubber band around the bundle of notes. Threw it across to Gobindo.

'There's three thousand. Enough for a portable TV.'

'A TV for the club, boss?'

'Or what? Since everyone's rushing about yelling fraudery and fakery, I'm not bloody hanging on to any of that money. Oh, and Koka, here's another four hundred. For booze.'

'Four hundred will get us twenty bottles, boss!'

'Twenty bottles! Fuck off! I'm not talking Bangla. I'm talking *English, English—Foreign Liquor Shop*.'

'What should I get, Herbert-da? Tonight seems to be a lion-league night!'

'One whisky, large. One rum, large. Ice, get three kilos, from New Market. For those who don't drink, get chops, chilli-hot chana, prawn cutlets, the ones with the sticking-out tails. Then salted peanuts, cigarettes—oof, I can't think of everything. You lot can't even learn how to spend the damn stuff! Tonight we're going to be mem-merry, femme-frothy.'

Herbert told them to come around 8.30. Then he fell asleep. Woke up at 7. Carried a chair to stand on and took down the sign from above his door. The one that read 'Conversations with the Dead. Prop: Herbert Sarkar'. Set it in a corner, its face turned to the wall. There'd been a new razor blade under the two books on the wall shelf. He checked to see it was still there. Then, pulling shut the door to his room, he went up to the first floor to meet his Jyathaima, she who'd married his father's older brother.

Jyathaima was engrossed in a TV show. Herbert stood beside her for a while, then silently came away. On a page in his notebook he scratch-scratched a few words, then tore it out and folded it away into his shirt pocket.

*

The booze bash was a smash hit.

The ice in the bucket was slowly turning to water. Herbert said, the fan will spread the cool air from the melting ice, cool the room. Herbert said, 'He scared the shit out of me. That Ghosh, that one who wrote the letter. How he was staring at me—bolshie-bloody bastard.

And only spurting English, only blurting English. The more the English, the more my balls shrinking and shrinking.'

'And that newspaper girl, boss—what a fucking cow! Puffing on her cigarettes one moment, flashing her camera the next!'

'Achha, Herbert-da, all this dialogue with the dead—was it all a load of crap?'

'What do you think?'

'If it was, then why did so many people come to you? So many people, so much talk—all crap?'

'I won't do this business any more, but. There's no stopping the stink that will spread, but Herbert Sarkar will pursue this line no longer.'

'Then what, boss?'

'I'm thinking. Thinking. A new line is bound to show up. Oh, and did you see, I took off the noticeboard outside? Now, Koka—show us something.'

Koka can show two things very well. One is an Isabgol ad, entitled Hanuman Shitting on a Chair Pot. This he'd picked up from TV. The other is Goju Bose's expression when he finally succeeded in signing up Krishanu and Bikash for Mohun Bagan.

'Which one, guru? Shit on a chair?'

'No, no—Goju Bose.'

Koka showed them. They freaked out. They flew high as kites. All the ice in the bucket turned to water. All the bottles grew empty, save a few drops of rum in one. By the time they got up to leave, Herbert was drawing close his windows.

Deep into the night, late into the darkness, to the house in the lane, the road in the house, the house in the street, the house back home, Borka had spoken those words:

'Let him sleep. He'll be all right if he sleeps.'

Two

Abroad, beloved, when you will travel
A new sight will greet you every day

—*Baldeb Palit*

From the notebook Herbert wrote in Puri while on holiday with his Jyathaima, we come to learn that:

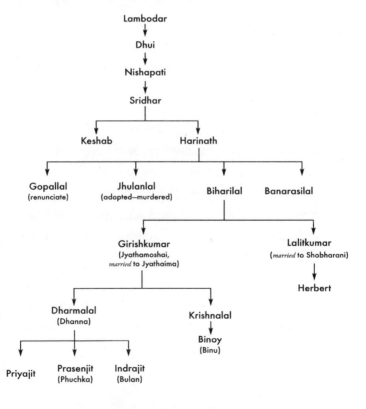

What we do not learn from the notebook is roughly as follows:

Herbert Sarkar. Father Lalitkumar. Mother Shobharani. Herbert's advent-arrival: 16 September 1949. Lalitkumar poured all his war-time earnings into the movies and was burbak-bankrupt fairly soon. In 1950, soon after Herbert's first birthday, Lalitkumar was khatam-killed in a jeep accident on the Darjeeling–Kurseong route, along with failed film actress Miss Ruby, two other passengers and the jeep driver. Mother Shobharani took baby Herbert and went to live with her parents. About eight months later, trying to hang the washing on a metal wire up on the terrace, Shobharani was electrocuted to death. Baby Herbert wailed, 'Ma go, Ma go' and tried to walk over to where she lay but stumbled and fell, and then lay on the ground, crying helplessly, until high in the sky he spotted two kites— a Burnface and a Splitbelly—engaged in a terrific slack-string fight which captured his attention entirely and thus saved his life. Baby Herbert then returned to his father's family home and proceeded, through indifference and neglect, towards adulthood, his Jyathaima being the only one to spare him some affection.

Jyathamoshai Girishkumar, Lalitkumar's older brother, had a whore habit. Which resulted in him contracting the inevitable disease, whose inevitable consequence was

a *general paralysis of the insane.* He would, as witnessed by
Herbert through his childhood, live on the first floor,
flit room-to-veranda and then back again, and on the
hour, every hour, with remarkable rooster-regularity, let
out a scream of 'Peeyu kahaan, peeyu kahaan!'

In the early days of this habit, if Jyathaima was in
the kitchen or, next to the ground-floor courtyard, in the
front-of-the-house bathroom, she would cry out a 'Here,
just coming dear' in response.

Girishkumar had two sons—Dharmalal, Herbert's
Dhanna-dada, and Krishnalal. Krishnalal was a professor
of English, extremely close to the progressive and undi-
vided Communist Party and still a believer. He taught
at the K. M. College in Baharampur and had managed
to build a small house for himself there. His share of the
Beadon Street paternal property, he had, after his son
Binu's death, written off to his brother Dhanna.

Dhanna, since his childhood, was a bundle of bas-
tardy, greedy as hell. Somehow, he'd managed to get a job
at the Mint. In those days, they were not so strict, and
maybe he'd indulged in some bribery too. Because every
day he'd come home with his tiffin box full of stolen
quarter-rupee shikis and half-rupee adhulis. By the time
he got caught, there was no way of telling for how long
he'd been stealing. Got fired, got jail time—although his
sentence was cut short quite a bit. Set free, Dhanna set

up a large lock-and-key shop in Naadu-babu's Bazar, got married and fathered three sons. The eldest lived in Gauhati. Fat and foolish, and a slave to his wife. But that one was still all right. The other two were lafanga-loafers—fatter and fattest, scoundrels to the core. One installed a satellite dish on the roof and supplied the neighbourhood with cable-TV connections—Star TV, MTV, BBC, people were gorging on that stuff these days. The other had conned a black belt into being his business partner and ran a kung-fu/karate school, although he knew fuck-all about any of it.

Dhanna-dada's wife was a clever woman, an *English-medium* girl. She ran a cookery class at home—a three-month *snacks* course that went from *Party Loaf* to *Ribbon Sandwich* as well as another three-month Mughlai course that included *Rainbow Polao, Murgh Irani*. She also baked *birthday cakes* to order.

Many wives came to Dhanna-dada's wife's classes.

From Herbert's room at the mouth of the lane, a room out and away from the house, he could, alas, not watch the women come and go.

But two lines in his notebook are dedicated to this affair:

> In Dhanna-dada's hall
> Mrs Centipedes coo and crawl

Herbert Sarkar. Admitted to Nandakumar Institution in Class Three and then, after his promotion from Class Five to Class Six, dropping out. Preferring to stay at home and reading whatever he could. That Herbert was no longer attending school escaped everyone's notice for quite a few months. By the time his Jyathaima did notice, she had already gotten used to sending him to the grocer, to the market. Of course, even when he had been going to school, it had been with Dhanna-dada's tiffin, his cheat sheets and his books. Since Dhanna-dada cheated in all his subjects, he needed more books than usual. This neighbourhood had a long tradition of sneaking in answers to the students through the window. All the boys were local boys, so the teachers didn't mind. Over the last 31 years, only three students at Nandakumar Institution had slid as low as a Second Division.

When Herbert was 18, Jyathaima took him to Puri for a fortnight. Herbert carried along a notebook and a pen. They had put up at the ashram run by Bharat Sevashram Sangha. There, Herbert's poetic genius had blossomed in leaps and bounds. The Herbert who wrote upon his arrival in Puri:

> Beside Bengal is where the Oriyas stay
> The Puri Express goes there every day

that same Herbert wrote, four days later:

A wave comes in
And out it goes
Here by the sea
Life ebbs and flows

And then, three days later, the more complex:

Mighty the wind when it blows on land
But evil when it blows on sea
Scaring even the octopus, who thinks,
'Oh, what will become of me?'

Herbert paid regular visits to the neighbourhood tailor to read the Bengali newspaper. To the *saloon*, to read *Morning Star* and *New Wave*.

His sense of rhythm and depth of perception had hinted at a luminous future although, in the end, it had all come to nought.

Back home from Puri, Herbert had written:

The hat-headed nuliya has a good life
No need to dress up and cut a dash
Splash in the ocean all day long,
Simply splash in the water and pocket the cash.

The diminution of poetic sense and poetic skill— Herbert was a dead example of that too. Who would not be mortified by the thought that the hand that had penned these earlier gems had also written this?

> Footpath, foot-fart
> Toots–plat–toots
> Dhanna goes to work
> In his gumboots.

Or this?

> How hot it is, oo
> Roach in my ear goes coo

After this stupendous stupidity, although it was *vulgar-very*, in this next ode to a motley of maids getting wet in the rain, one finds one's faith restored, albeit slightly:

> Ladies, why do you wet, oh?
> Wet so
> Girls, why grow wet, low?
> Come, lo.

In the end, what arouses not only despair but also pity is the passing off—in a fit of desperation, clearly—of Amrik Singh Arora's lyrics as his own (these are the last lines in his notebook):

> Let me be
> The kohl so black in your silver kohl container.

*

Dhanna-dada's house was not too large, not too small. A two-storey house, a terrace. On the terrace, a room used for prayers, and a smaller terrace atop that. On it, a tank that once had water pumped straight from the Ganga. Now, it had a Star-TV satellite dish. A small room on the ground floor—not towards the main door but to the back. Used to store old books, 78 RPM records, documents and the electricity meter. When in 1969 Binu came to Calcutta to study, a small bed and a table fan had been put in for him. After his death, the room lay locked up for a few years. Then one day it became Herbert's office and, until his last moment, was his room.

Before that, Herbert had slept on the first-floor veranda, the one that ran inside the house. And that stayed dry even in the monsoons. His clothes hung on a line along the stairs that led up to the terrace. Once there'd been a ruinous-rotten wooden staircase leading up from the ground floor to the terrace-room top-terrace. But as you climbed up it, you could peek into the neighbours' bedrooms. Their loud protests had rendered that staircase practically defunct. A few days after Binu died, there was a huge storm. In the middle of that rainy night, the bottom half of the staircase collapsed. In the morning they found the top half hanging from the terrace-top, refusing to let go. Only after much prodding and pulling, yanking and yelling, did it finally fall to the ground.

At the crossroads in front of the house, they celebrated Kali Puja. They celebrated Durga Puja too, but that was a little farther off. Where Bachha-da had his sweet shop. Same sweets all year around, but for Dol he made Dol Delights.

An album of photographs belonging to Lalitkumar should have come to Herbert by way of his inheritance. In it, colour photographs, from the early years, of Rudolf Valentino, Lon Chaney (in various roles), Douglas Fairbanks, Charlie Chaplin, Greta Garbo, Lilian Gish, Mary Pickford and Errol Flynn, to some from the later eras, to Clark Gable, Robert Taylor, Van Heflin, Humphrey Bogart, Bette Davis, Vivien Leigh, Katharine Hepburn. Then: Lalitkumar and Shobharani in front of a Sunbeam Talbot automobile. Lalitkumar flanked by Madhu Bose and Sadhana Bose. Failed film actress Miss Ruby and Lalitkumar. Shobharani and Herbert. Baby Herbert.

Bur Herbert never laid eyes on the album. Because Dhanna had pinched it, wrapped it in some old clothes and stashed it away at the bottom of his cupboard.

Lalitkumar had amassed another collection—cigarette holders. Those were lopat-looted not by Dhanna, alas, but by someone else. Dhanna had looked everybloodywhere but never managed to locate the cigar box in which Lalitkumar lovingly hoarded them. Thanks to Lalitkumar's wicked ways of the West, Dhanna was able to steal, now and then, his imported cigarettes and his Scotch. Now and then, some money too. Lalitkumar was not the sort of man who ever kept count. So he never noticed the pilfering. Beyond a shadow of doubt, had Lalitkumar not blown away on the movies his immense-incredible war-time fortune made from scrap iron and copper, Herbert's life story would have been very different indeed.

Herbert Sarkar. Five feet six inches tall. Fair. Features sharp, build Caucasian. Slim. Lalitkumar must have felt that, somewhere, the boy had a Hollywood-ish air, a Leslie Howard-ish air. So the boy got a shahebi name—Herbert. Herbert's mother was a practically pure-white beauty, bred in the shaded-shadowy homes of North Calcutta. Lalitkumar himself was no less dashing and debonair. Anyway, no matter how, Herbert's manner was always a bit hero-hero-ish. This Western movie-star effect was heightened by the fact that he spent most of his time living in fear. The fear drained the blood from his face and made him paler-palest, hence fairer-fairest. Because of his mother and father, he lived in fear of cars and electricity. Then the fear of Dhanna's thrashings. The fear of Jyathamoshai's sudden cock-crows of 'Peeyu kahaan! Peeyu kahaan!'

And the entirely new kind fear that Binu later brought with him.

*

When he was 14, Herbert had an extraordinary experience. One afternoon, rummaging through the heap of old books in that last room, he discovered an old tin trunk. In it lay a human skull and some long-ish bones. No one in this family tree's any tendril or tangent had ever studied medicine. Nor magic. Unprepared for the sight of them, Herbert had at first been terrified by the skull, the eyeless sockets, the teeth. But in time, time and time again, Herbert would open the trunk and stare at the skull and bones. Try to imagine the man they had been. No matter who, an overwhelming sadness for him would engulf Herbert.

Two years later, Herbert put the skull and bones into a little cloth bag, and then went to the Old Ganga behind Keoratala Crematorium and threw them into the water.

He used to store his own things in the trunk, later. Later, his money too.

After immersing the remains of that unfortunate unknown, Herbert was filled with an intoxicating attraction for death. He would feel that he was drowning in the darkness of those empty eye sockets, that all around him spun a Ferris wheel of stars or a furious flutterment of fireflies.

Soon after, he began to read and reread those aforementioned two most important books.

Soon after, his friend Khororobi committed *suicide*. Herbert was 19. The boy had a khor-kutter, a straw-cutting machine, at home, so his friends had stuck 'khor' before his name, the name his parents had chosen for their son, Sun. Robi. Hence, Khororobi. Straw Sun. Khororobi was a good boy. Who had fallen deeply in love with the short Jaya from the neighbourhood behind theirs. Every evening, Jaya and a gaggle of girlfriends would step out for a walk, come over and chat with the girls on this side. That Khororobi would begin to act honey-funny whenever he saw Jaya, that everyone knew. Everyone also knew that he didn't have the balls—he'd never dare to venture out of their gang. But that fateful Ashtami day, what madness filled his head, that only he knew. Elbowing his way through the crazy crowds, he strode into Jaya's neighbourhood Durga Puja and handed her a slip of paper and one of those teeny-tiny fountain pens that had then flooded the market. On the paper was scrawled in a crow-leg-and-stork-leg script: 'Jaya, an offering at your devi-divine feet from a humble devotee. Yours, Robi.'

The local boys grab-nabbed him red-handed. Jaya sped-fled back home. Khororobi somehow struggled free. The scuffle had ripped apart his new shirt. That night, Jaya's uncle came to have a word at Khororobi's house. The two neighbourhoods grew dense with hostility. Nabami, Dashami—Khororobi was AWOL. Then, the strains of the idol immersions not yet past when, in the late afternoon of the day after, a hue and cry and why-why-why. Khororobi had been found. Floating in the wall-encircled Corporation pond. Dead.

Khororobi's corpse floated face down near the water's western edge, floated in water two-men deep, floated and bobbed and swayed and rocked. On the shore stood all the neighbourhood boys, stood Herbert. The sunlight shone on the water, made it a little transparent, one could see beneath the surface a waggle of waterweeds and then the deep green of the moss thickening into darkness. On the shore, a bicycle. Someone holds out a shaft of bamboo. Two boys from the swimming club get into the water. A prod from the bamboo upturns Khororobi and sets him floating away from the diving board and into murky waters. The sun is swiftly sliding. The police have arrived. Striding to the pond, the sergeant asks, 'Corpse come up?' No one answers. The swimmers have reached Khororobi. But as soon as they touch him, he floats away, bobs away on the backs of many little waves. Then each boy swims to one side and grabs a fistful of shoulder shirt. Khororobi is finally caught. Then they kick and kick their way to shore, and the water stretches taut and tight Khororobi's full head of hair.

Herbert looks at him by the dying afternoon light and thinks that Khororobi is coming back as a dutiful and duly obedient school of fish.

That scene, it could have been a photograph.

Although by now it would have yellowed, corner-nibbled and slur-blurred with time. Yet, for a hundred years hence, and a hundred years more, by the light of the moon, in the mists of a winter morning, Khororobi and his love will remain afloat on those still waters of death. Around him will twist and tumble mermaids, the ones who cry but whose tears you cannot see.

*

'My name is Herbert! I'm a tit. You've seen a tit. Now see a tat.'

'On the velvet greens of grass and flower, houri-fairies prance and play.'

'Kite, *aeroplane*, *balloon*, broom, man, parachute, bird—they all fall down. Yet first they rise. This also rises. This also falls.'

'If man is 1, then 0 is dead man. Man + dead man = 1 + 0 = 1 = Khororobi.'

'Water's riddle in cranny and crack
Fate's flight of fancy in saree edged with black.'
—Herbert

Three

Life, dear god, is hell!

—*Maankumari Basu*

Rabba! Rabba!

That kite, that one, with its sun-smeared belly, rising high, fly-high-ing higher, if you turned away for a moment as it began to fall, there, th–e–e–e–r-e, on the other side of the 13-storey building until just the other day you could see the Howrah Bridge . . . the top of the Victoria Memorial . . . there, shaheb-para, the posh neighbourhood . . . there, cinema-para, where all the movie theatres were . . . there, the telephone office at New Market . . . closer home, the Seal housetop . . . then the rowdy Pals' terrace . . . the clothes of the Christian landlord's Punjabi tenants drying in the sun . . . then the sigh-soaked Haldar terrace where Buki, beautiful, dust-skinned, soft, slightly saucy-breasted Buki would come no more in the evenings, home from school, walking from one side of the terrace to the other and back again, an open book in her hands, the potted plants in the terrace garden swooning in the breeze, the strands of Buki's hair lifting and shifting, the pages of her book furling and uncurling . . .

The terrace-room top-terrace was Herbert's true place. That was where he had perceived everything. The extraordinary dream that had granted him social status and standing, that had granted him fame—but that had also, in the end, been his end—that dream too had come to him there.

The Ganga-water tank used to be on the top-terrace. Once upon a time, Herbert would climb in and, scratch-scrabbling in the fine mud at its bottom, catch little white shrimps, their legs stir-whirring the water as they tried to flee.

Round snails clung to its sides.

Later, the water stopped. The mud dried. The pipe broke.

Later, rainwater collected in it. Then, in it, at most a little moss or scum or a clutch of bubbles bursting into somersaulting water-mites or mosquito-spawn. Without the flow of Ganga water, the tank was dead. But to Herbert even the dead tank had its uses. In the hot summer months, he would slide his way under it and sleep in its shade. Take his pickles or lozenges there. Suck on a lozenge a few times, then put it on a scrap of paper, and read *Accounts of the Afterlife*. Read and read and then fall asleep. Waking up, if he found three or four—

no more would venture up to the top—ants had begun to nibble at the lozenge, he would flick them off, one by one, and then suck on the lozenge again.

Another kind of insect, many-legged and mild, lived in the cracks of that top-terrace. There were perhaps in all of India and the world no insect so nonviolent and peaceful.

That time in Calcutta, when lakh-lakh locusts had swooped upon the city, Herbert had been astonished at the sound of them smash-crashing against the tank. How different that sound was from the sound of rain!

In winter, Herbert would climb up to that sun-warmed top-terrace, wearing the sweater from Krishna-dada and the *wrapper* from Jyathaima.

Every year, long before Vishwakarma Puja, would start the season of kites. One of those days, Herbert was fast asleep on the empty top-terrace. Suddenly, something slid across his stomach. Opening his eyes, he found a strand of string severed from a kite. The infant Herbert, lying not too far from his dead mother's body, had witnessed, up in the sky, a slack-stringed struggle between two kites. Even though he did not remember it, he felt a terrible tug for the slack-stringed fight. But for a slack-string fight, one needed a reel full of string. Because you had to let loose let fly lengths and lengths of it, because if you ran out of the glass-glazed manja string, if you got to the reel-end plain white string, then you were bound to lose.

To twist and pull off a tight-string fight, you needed more *violence*. Then, if there wasn't a strong enough breeze, the kite seemed to mutter-stutter through clenched teeth the frustrated thoughts of its owner. Herbert used to stare, incredulous, at those thrust-and-destroy contests—kite-kidnap games being fought in mid-air, as though the flyers were reel-feeling the throb and thrill of rape.

What Herbert loved most, though, was to see, at *high altitude*, a loose kite drifting off on its own. If it seemed to topsy-turvy a lot, then one knew it had been severed right beneath the tail. That it barely had any string left. And if it seemed to proceed at a stately pace, rolling like a heavy coin, then one knew it had a lot of string to it still, that it would bring good luck both to its captor and its new reel.

Dhanna's three sons used to fly kites from the big terrace. The small terrace higher up was forbidden to them. If Herbert ever caught a kite up in his high place, he gave it to them.

The Gayla, the Candle, the Bird King, the Four Square, the Splitbelly, the Badge, the Chessboard, the Burnface, the Betel Leaf—no matter how gaily glorious they were, the deep-dark Booloom was the king of kites.

Once, he'd seen a severed black Booloom floating across a clouded sky and been almost afraid. Never before nor after had he seen such a solemn-sombre final journey. As a matter of fact, even his own final journey had not been so grim with gravity.

It was on that same top-terrace that Herbert, one day in his youth, felt erupting from his body an incredible elation and sensual satisfaction. In his eyes, then, the darkness of the sun. And around him, the foot and a half-tall terrace walls gleaming with deep green moss.

From that same top-terrace, for so many years, Herbert had watched in the evenings the cranes fly back home in long lines across the sky. Small bats swooping when darkness first fell. And the large bats that emerged when that darkness thickened into night. Aeroplane lights flickering. In the blink of an eye, from the countless constellations, one star slips and falls. A kite-balloon bobs past. Herbert had even seen a kite-lantern once— a paper packet made stiff with a frame, a candle placed inside, and all of it then tied to a kite and flown in the air. Once he'd held on to a kite-balloon until the string went taut in his hands.

*

As a boy, Herbert had gone with his Krishna-dada to a screening of *Fall of Berlin* organized by the Communist Party. Then to many others, mostly war documentaries.

Once he'd seen a block of ice upturning, and the soldiers on it twirl-swirling their way to the bottom of the bottomless sea. No one bothered to tell him he was watching Eisenstein's *Alexander Nevsky*. Long before that, once, at Indira, he'd watched a Bengali movie in which Sabitri Chatterjee stood in the courtyard of her husband's home, holding her slippers upon her head. And during the Durga Puja in the neighbourhood, he'd watched, among others, *Morning Will Come Again*.

Later, when he began to earn, he'd been begged to rent videos by the neighbourhood nut jobs, and ended up watching even more many more movies.

But of all the things he had learnt, if half had been from those aforementioned two most important books, then the rest had surely been from that top-terrace.

It was from that top-terrace that Buki and Herbert had been drawn to each other. Every evening, Buki would come up to her terrace. Herbert would, of course, be on his terrace already. Then, a few moments of deep closeness, despite the two-house gap between them. Until when Buki arrived, until then her frocks drying in the sun would keep Herbert company.

Buki went to and fro school in a rickshaw. Buki and her family were tenants at the Haldar house. For about two years. Then they left. Herbert was 16, Buki 11. The Saraswati Puja not long before they left, that afternoon, by the side of the local library room, that was when they first spoke to each other. Almost invisible, hiding behind the pillar of the Banerjee-house gate, Herbert had whispered. 'If I write you, will you read?'

Buki had nodded, yes.

'Which class are you in?'

'Six. You?'

'I study. But not at school.'

'You have a tutor?'

Herbert had nodded, yes. Hating himself for nodding, yes.

After Buki went away, Herbert spent quite a few months away from the top-terrace. Although later he went back, went again. Saw how the shadows thickened at evening end, how a light or two came on before all the rest, how the smoke from the clay ovens flowed away like rivers. Saw how a little after that, how the terrace didn't feel so empty any more. Perhaps at the heart of that indistinct impossible stood Buki, waving, smiling. It seemed that way even if he rubbed his eyes for a second look. Although the eyes are known to be blurred-over at times like that.

Later, when the Haldars built their third floor, then Buki's terrace was lost.

On one of the walls of his own top-terrace, Herbert had scratched a B with a bit of brick. Scratched it deep. And even when it was grownover with moss, Herbert could tell that neathunder it the B was looking at him, that it was nodding, yes.

*

That little top-terrace had never betrayed Herbert. Although two things had happened that could have proved dangerous. One evening, it was pouring rain pouring down, and Herbert was stuck up there. So heavy and strong the rain. And so loud the sound of the hailstones hitting the tank. Herbert dived under it for shelter. A few hailstones bounced off the ground and landed near him. Flashes of lightning. Crashes of thunder. A few bolts landing with a sky-splitting crack. Herbert was frightened he'd never get down. Couldn't get down. It was raining that hard. What if he lost his bearings? What if he stepped off in mid-air above the street or the lane below?

The other time, it had been the morning of Kali Puja. Someone had been testing the flying firecrackers. One of those red-hot clay encasings flew onto the top-terrace—and exploded.

On Herbert's neck, right below his chin, right on his throat, there was, until the end, a little white scar.

*

Dhanna-dada, Dhanna-boudi, their three growing sons—Herbert drifted further and farther away from them.

The deeply thinking-thoughtful walk in half-an-hour-away shahebi Victoria Square and the attendant shahebi affectations—all that had come later. But the start of those expeditions lay in a winter morning of the mid-1980s, when Jyathaima gave Herbert his Jyatha-moshai's Ulster overcoat. Even though it was moth-eaten in places, even though its nap had rubbed off in places, even though its belt was lost—even then, Dhanna-dada complained within earshot of his mother: 'All the old-is-gold things in the house, all the best-most things in the house, all that she shoves into the belly of that squat-and-eat-for-nothing. A father's prized possession! And she never thought once to ask the eldest son!'

'Dhanna, half-old man you've become, still as greedy as a goat. So keen about your share, a son's share, eh? So what do you care if I give him that coat? Would you ever wear it?'

'Look, Ma, don't would-you-how-could-you about things you don't understand. Do you think I'm being selfish about that coat? No, I'm more bothered about habits. He gets food, he gets clothes. He gets this and that. On top of all that if today you get him a parrot, and tomorrow a cockatoo—where's it all going to stop, eh?

Then he'll want his share of the house, want a house and homefront of his own. Then?'

'That he never asks for because he's such a good boy. And why shouldn't he? His father left him a share, after all!'

'There, see, now, see, you're making me lose my temper, see? Bugger his father's share. Do you think there's brain enough in that skull to even calculate a share? There's balls enough in that body? Ask for his share! He's certainly asking for his share!'

'If he asks, what'll you say?'

'What say? I'll thrash him black and blue and throw him out. All these years of feeding and clothing—let's add that up first. I'll carve a canal through the motherfucker.'

The minds of those persons who are sensual materialists are incapable of understanding the afterlife. Why only the afterlife—they are incapable of understanding so many subtle sensations of this life too. Those minds revolve around thoughts of the body, its sensual pleasures, and its desires, nay, are obsessed with such thoughts and thus dwell in a state of perpetual restlessness. Hence, the highest realization, the purest truth-thought about the afterlife cannot

manifest itself in those minds. Those things
that the mind can concentrate upon, from those
it can extract joy. Those things upon which it
cannot so concentrate, from those it can extract
nothing. This inherent property, this innate
characteristic of the human mind is known to
man and boy alike.

—*Mysteries of the Afterlife*

*

After the Ulster episode, Herbert's two nephews,
Prasenjit (Phuchka) and Indrajit (Bulan) suddenly
attacked him one day in the ground-floor dining room.
Their excuse was that while they had been studying,
Herbert had been chopping up old coconut shells for
kindling, deliberately making a racket to disturb them.
Jyathaima was then upstairs, in her prayer room. She
could hear nothing. Dhanna was out, in his shop. Boudi
was not home either. The eldest son, Priyajit, was in the
bath. Hearing Herbert's screams of pain, he'd rushed out
with only a towel round his waist and shouted at his
brothers to stop. By then Herbert's lip was split wide
open. And bleeding. The skin beneath his eyes was puffy
and swollen. His teeth were throbbing.

There was another witness to this event—Dhanna-
dada's maid, Nirmala.

When Herbert was out in the courtyard, washing the blood from his mouth, when Priyajit was pouring him water, then his head was spinning, then, he remembers, up above him, his Jyathamoshai roaring. 'Peeyu kahaan! Peeyu kahaan!'

Thanks to this incident, the deeply despairing Herbert succeeded in securing the key to the gates of heaven. At the tailor's, he'd told Dulal and Rakhal-babu that he'd slipped and fallen in the courtyard. But via Nirmala, the truth soon seeped out into the neighbourhood ears. At the tube well, at the grocer's, at the sweet shop—everywhere and to everyone, Nirmala said, 'Those heartless boys, oh! That good-man uncle of theirs, how could they thrash him like that?' Word spread so far so fast that one day, in front of so many people, Barilal, the eldest of the Ganguly brothers actually spoke to Dhanna about it: 'Dhanna! What's going on in that house of yours? Never heard such things in this neighbourhood before. Nephews beating up their uncles?'

The local boys, even the *junior gang* who greeted him with cries of 'Titbird'—they stopped their teasing and drew closer to him to express their sympathy. And because they drew closer, stood nearer, the nephews realized they were cornered.

Just as this incident brought Herbert close to the hearts of many, so too another incident took place to understand which one will, of course, have to rely upon an elaborately esoteric explanation. The blows that rained upon his head, both front and back, must have jostled Herbert's still-solidifying *brain*, or else how could a memory from fifteen years ago come to him so suddenly, slipped into the envelope of such an extraordinary dream? This intervention of nature led the story of Herbert's life around a new bend in the road, and—even though it may have been pure coincidence—what was cause for abundant astonishment was that the father of killed-by-a-police-bullet-in-1971 Binu, the father of Herbert's Naxalite nephew Binu, Herbert's Krishnadada had come to Calcutta for some work and was, in fact, at that very moment, in that very house.

> I said, 'Look, Dinanath, yesterday's incident must have been preying upon your mind. Hence, those terrible scenes playing across your dreams. Now come, everyone, try and sleep in peace.'
>
> 'What, sir, did you just say?' roared Dinanath. 'Are you calling me a liar? Dismissing my words as mere dream? I do not lie—I did not dream. All that I told you I saw with my own eyes. If you do not believe me, ask them. We could surely not all have been dreaming the same dream!'
>
> —'The Horribly Haunted Circus'

*

But oh woe, where is Buki gone? On that terrace now sits only a Star TV satellite dish. Herbert gone. Soviet Union gone. Hippodrome Circus gone. The famous Dinu Hotel beside the Gosain house on Simla Street gone. 'Since the eyes of the great and gracious Sri Sureshchandra Basu were always-almost closed, everyone called him the Grand Great Shut Eye.'

He's gone, too.

Rabba! Rabba!

Four

Hark! Hark! The trumpet blows,
the trumpet!

—*Rangalal Bandyopadhyay*

Binoy, aka Binu, came to Calcutta to study Geology Honours at Asutosh College. Many years ago, when Herbert was a little boy, Binu had taught him a rhyme: 'Copsticks, broom-sticks, nothing scares the *Comminists.*' Binu moved into that room by the street, that room at the back of the house. Krishnalal had come with him, to settle him in. A bed was bought. A mattress. Jyathaima brought down the bundle of bed linen hanging from the roof of the first-floor veranda, and took him a pillow.

Slowly, a Winchell Holmes, and then many other shaheb-written volumes, filled the shelves carved into the wall.

Binu. Serious. Average height and build. Sweet of speech.

One morning—it must have been around nine—Binu was stretched out on his stomach in bed, a pillow tucked under his chest, writing something. Herbert opened the door a crack and peeped in. Binu looked up and smiled. 'Herbert-kaka! What are you looking at? Come in, come in.'

Herbert and Binu grew quite close. Herbert liked Binu's friends too. They would let him have the odd cigarette. Chat with him. But then would come a time when Binu would say, 'Herbert-kaka, now, if you don't mind . . .' And Herbert would realize that Binu was asking him to leave them alone for a bit. But he didn't mind that, for Binu was never rude.

Binu had bought him a *full pant*. And a *belt*.

'Oof, Herbert-kaka, just like an American filmstar!'

Dhanna got a bit of a shock when he saw those pants. Later, he was even more shocked to hear that Binu was the one who'd bought them, with money saved up from his *tuitions*.

'See?' said Jyathaima, 'Look and learn a little. Not everyone is a miser like you!'

'Oof!' said Dhanna-dada, 'stop your scratch-scratch! Learn what, tell me, from all this show-show of love? But yes, the ones who could look and learn are my younger boys—no studying, no manners between the two of them.'

'Peeyu kahaan!' said Jyathamoshai, 'Peeyu kahaan!'

*

To hereafter-obsessed Herbert, Binu had provided a different definition of death.

'What's all that mumbo-jumbo you read? Nonsense. *Ridiculous!* He died, went off a ghost, she died, came back a ghost—all these pages scrawling-crawling with ghosts, tell me, have *you* ever seen even one? It's not as if people aren't dying all the time. Why, in this house alone, who knows how many deaths there've been.'

'Just because I haven't seen one doesn't mean it's all lies.'

'Not only you—no one has seen one.'

'Then what about the *planchettes*?'

'What about them? I was there for one in Baharampur.'

'You were? And?'

'And what? And nothing. The ones who do it are the ones pushing the glass or shaking the pencil. Although, of course, I don't blame you. As long as a handful of men can keep fooling the greater millions into working for them till they die, can keep cheating them, for just as long will thrive your ghosts and ghouls, your gods and goddesses, your dharma and karma. Listen, listen to this.' (Binu opens a small book, turns a few pages):

' "Countless revolutionary martyrs have laid down their lives in the interests of the people, and our hearts are filled with pain as we the living think of them—can there be any personal interest, then, that we would not sacrifice or any error that we would not discard?"—Do you know who's words these are?'

Herbert shakes his head. He has no idea.

'Mao Tse-Tung.'

*

The night of 19 November 1970 was the night of the bloody Barasat killings. The night when Jatin Das, Kanai Bhattacharya, Sankar Chattopadhyay, Samir Mitra, Swapan Pal, Samirendranath Dutta, Tarun Das and Ganesh Ghatak were killed by the police in cold blood.

Charu Majumdar, General Secretary, Communist Party of India (Marxist–Leninist), sent out a call in his communiqué dated 22 November 1970:

> Today the most sacred task of every Indian is to rouse the intensest hatred for all these cowards, imperialism's running-dogs and assassins. This is today the demand of our countrymen—the demand of patriotism.
>
> Every revolutionary cadre should take the resolve to avenge the heroic martyrs. These butchers are enemies of the Indian people, enemies of progress and lackeys of foreigners. The Indian people will not be liberated until these butchers are liquidated.

Binu heard the call and sprang to action. Some nights he wouldn't come home.

Dhanna-dada's neighbourhood, though, was a completely Congress one. Even if a few red drops remained, they were barely visible.

And Barilal was an informer.

One day, Binu sent Herbert with quite a lot of money, and a receipt book printed with pictures of Mao Tse-Tung and Lin Pao, to be delivered to one Bijoy in the Lake Market area. Bijoy then took him to Kalighat, to a spot behind the Greek Church. There, a man wearing glasses, stubble-chinned and sunken-cheeked, embraced Herbert and said, 'Congratulations, comrade! Binu has told me a lot about you. We need more loyal friends like you. Have some tea.'

On the way back, two boys helped him negotiate the Manohorpukur crossing. Somewhere, somewhere close, a bomb exploded.

Herbert never came to know that in 1971, on the morning of 9 May, when Bijoy was hiding in Baranagar, when Bijoy crept out to buy some food, when Bijoy was standing at a small shop in the market, then Bijoy was shot dead by the police.

Binu had not been back home for a long spell. Dhanna-dada sent off a letter to Krishnalal, Binu's father.

Krishnalal wrote back:

Binu is a young man now. He knows what he is doing. And he is not alone in this, for there are many others like him who too have arrived at such knowledge and such a decision. Therefore, there is no question at all of my asking him to stop. Binu's mother, too, entertains an agreement with my opinion. However, I understand that this is posing a difficulty for the household. So I am thinking of other arrangements. But I will have to request some time until I can be in Calcutta again.

I hope Baba and Ma are well.

To Herbert and to your sons, my . . .

But Krishnalal did not have to come to make other arrangements, after all.

One night, on Elgin Road, on the walls of the ship-shaped house, when three boys were using a stencil to paint the face of Mao Tse-Tung, then one of the men sleeping on the pavement on the other side of the street had removed the sheet from his face and fired. One boy, standing on the shoulders of the other two, was painting. That boy fell. The other two tried to drag him away. But the air grew thick with the sound of running feet. The air grew shrill with the sound of blowing whistles. At the request of the wounded boy, the other two left him and fled. The wounded boy tried to drag himself along on his belly, scrape himself along by his elbows.

A few yards. At most.

The pavement was streaked with blood.

Then he lost consciousness.

Sub-Inspector Santosh realized: *Prize-catch*! If Binoy could be helped to live, he would be helped to spill a lot of beans. So, a *cabin* at PG Hospital. A doctor.

'The lungs are *punctured*. Nothing to be done. Any time. Tell the family if you know them.'

The family was told. Dhanna-dada sent a telegram to Krishnalal. Herbert spent all his time at hospital. Even though he lost most of his blood between the pavement and the floor of the police van, an indomitable life-force kept Binu alive for another forty-eight hours.

Krishnalal arrived.

In the meantime, the police ransacked Binu's room, overturned the mattress, upturned the books—but found nothing. Long before this, acting upon Binu's instructions, Herbert had carried up to his top-terrace copies of *The Patriot* and *The Southern Country*; a Bengali manual on guerrilla warfare printed in Chattogram; recipes for Molotov cocktail painstakingly cut out of the *Tricontinental*, a Cuban magazine; *The Red Book*; some letters. And burnt them all. Little by little, bit by bit. To keep the smoke to a minimum.

No one had noticed a thing.

At the hospital, Professor Prafullakanti, Krishnalal's friend, took him downstairs for a cup of tea.

In a sudden burst of benevolence, one of the two armed guards outside Binu's door told Herbert, 'Go in, he's delirious. Now, where's that damn father of his?'

Herbert went in. To Binu. A blanket drawn up to his chest. An upside-down bottle with a rubber tube ending in his arm. And something else, something that Herbert could not see. From under the blanket, near his feet, a chain. Looped around the iron bed-leg twice and then secured with a lock. Once a young man had escaped despite the *traction*-clamp-contraption tight around his neck. Hence, now this more *foolproof* arrangement.

Binu's eyes were closed but his lips were moving. And what had sounded like delirium to the policeman was in fact lines from a poem by Barasat martyr Samir Mitra, remembered with great thought and uttered— not necessarily recited—with great effort. . .

I can see
Before my eyes, this forever-familiar world
Changing, changing . . .

('Changing,' Binu said, 'changing, changing.' Then the next few words had been remembered, then something like a cough had rattled him, then at the edge of his lips drops of blood had flecked the froth-foam that burbled, then Herbert reached for the blood-dotted towel near his pillow, then the nurse rushed in, then the nurse wiped Binu's mouth, then the nurse rushed out of the room.)

Ravaged, ruined, and ransacked, dust to dust
The old days fall.
A storm is coming.

('Coming,' Binu said, 'coming, coming.' Then opened wide open his eyes. Then Herbert leant in, leant closer. Then Herbert's eyes were full of tears. Then Binu's eyes looked left and right and here and there. Then Binu hadn't been looking for anyone—then Binu had been looking to see if there were any policemen in the room.)

'Yes, Binu, what is it?'

'Herbert-kaka, prayer room, diary . . . Herbert . . . kaka . . . diary . . . behind Kali . . . diary . . .' Then Binu stared. At nothing. People don't usually stare that way. Not hoping to see anything, but staring anyway.

The doctor came in. Told Herbert to step aside. The police. The nurse.

Expired.

Then, via police protocol and the morgue, to the crematorium. Binu's body slid into the electric furnace. So late at night, but so many policemen still on guard. His eyes fixed on the furnace, Krishna-dada mutter-murmuring.

Above the furnace door, someone had scrawled, 'Police dog, Debi Roy, Beware!—CPI(M–L).'

A certain intellectual police officer told a certain subordinate, 'Look, look, a Naxal's father, burning his son and chanting his prayers.'

Herbert heard those words and moved closer to Krishna-dada. Tears streamed down his cheeks.

Krishna-dada was reciting:

Stormraisers every one, storm-hearted they,
  Writ in the blood of our foreign foes,
  In bullets and guns and bombs and blows
Their lives and stories thrill us even today.

Then, Binu was burning then.

*

Since then, the stinking and stagnant and wholly insignificant period that came to pass was so wearisome that we would be hard put to find its parallel in the annals of history. The sliver of the city in which Herbert lived had remained untouched by time from time immemorial but then the old houses were riven apart by shouting and screaming, and then shackled back together by walls and doors built up in the unlikeliest of places. And, yes, a change of taste had most certainly been provided by the promoters who tore down some of those ancient homes and replaced them with the new-fangled *multistoreyed*. Then, by the *video* shop—Gyanobaan and Buddhimaan had been the first to take the revolutionary step of setting it up. There was a *roll* shop too, at the mouth of the lane. The main road had once been lined with tall trees whose soft shadows would fall upon the double-decker buses like a cool caress. Now the trees were gone. Now, only the frantic frenzy of traffic. The pushcart men had a favourite resting spot in the neighbourhood—that was gone. Herbert remembered, one night there'd been an earthquake. The bundle of bed-linen hanging from the roof of the first-floor veranda—swinging like a *pendulum*. One of the old pushcart men started shouting 'Bhuidola, bhuidola!' in terror, trying to warn his sleeping friends. Yet, the next morning, on that *decadent* street, yesterday's gamblers and yesternight's drunks walking bleary eyed to the market, the lump-clumps of hair on the floor of the *saloon*, the rattle of the rickshaws—which man was man enough to tell from all this that just the night before this place had been rocked by an earthquake, a small one but still?

There had been a few elections, in those in-between years. Not that Herbert gave a damn. He never voted. Every election day, he refused to step out of the house and spent all day perched high on the top-terrace. In *tribute* to Binu.

Even though he could no longer remember much about him.

*

One afternoon, after the gift of the Ulster overcoat and the ugly thrashing from his nephews that followed, Herbert was up on the top-terrace, fast asleep. Krishna-dada had been visiting Calcutta, then. After Binu died, he'd written off his share of the house to Dhanna-dada and gone away. Binu's mother died about five years after her son. So Krishna-dada was back after almost 13–14 years. Just like all the other times, this time too Krishna-dada took Herbert to the Hawker's Corner and bought him two dhutis and two *full shirts*.

New-dhuti-and-new-shirt-clad Herbert was asleep. Streaks of sunlight shone through strands of feathery white clouds. A gentle breeze blew, like a moist breath upon the skin.

And Herbert dreamt a dream:

What revelry is this, that you don a human part
Are they, then, so close to your heart?

—*Nagendrabala Mustafi*

Enormous, endless, a curtain of glass. On this side, running along its length, a broken-battered dirt track. On

that side, at the base of a golden mountain, a vast cave
from whose ceiling hang slivers of stone, like a crystal
chandelier, from whose floor rise rivulets of rock—
Herbert can hear Binu's voice clearly—the ones that
hang from the roof are *stalactites*, the ones that rise from
the ground are *stalagmites*—that's right, Binu had pointed
them out in a book. Then the mountain comes to an end.
Walking on, walking on and on. Sometimes, on the other
side of the glass, water. Sometimes, sky. The light is
fading. It's such a long way back. Back where? As soon as
this fear touches his heart, a cloud of countless crows col-
lects on the other side. Pecking. Flapping. But making
no sound.

Crow blood and crow shit slowly smear-soil the
glass.

Then, through a gap in the crow-cumulus, Herbert
sees Binu.

The middle of the 1980s. After Binu's death, this is
the first Binu.

Binu standing still. Binu saying something. Waves
of crows wash over him, hide him from view. At the foot
of the glass, on the other side, crow corpses fall and fes-
ter. Binu comes closer. Binu smiles. Herbert smiles back.
Waves. The words, Binu's words, echoing on this side,
stained with the strains of a song from a distant loud-
speaker ...

'Herbert-kaka, prayer room, diary . . . Herbert . . . kaka . . . diary behind Kali's picture . . . diary . . .'

Binu is close to the glass. Binu is staring. People don't usually stare that way. Not hoping to see anything, but staring anyway.

Herbert sat up with a start. Swiped his shirt-cuff across his mouth and wiped away the dream-dribble. Raised his sleepy eyes to the sky and saw a rainbow. Saw what looked like people walking over that rainbow. The sound of the heart-train thundering. The sound of the city blundering about.

Herbert came down. Not to the prayer room. But straight to the first-floor veranda. Jyathaima was sitting on a mat on the floor. Krishna-dada, Dhanna-dada and Dhanna-boudi were drinking tea. Dhanna was about to say something when Herbert rushed in, screaming: 'Jyathaima! I had a dream! Binu came. He said . . .'

(Then he was confused. But then he remembered, shifting and faint . . .)

Krishna-dada smiled. 'You saw Binu in a dream?'

Then he remembered everything.

'See? How could I see? So many crows I could barely see. Binu, Binu said—come, come with me, Jyathaima . . .'

'Calm down,' Dhanna-dada said, 'then tell us. It's easy to get confused. A dream, after all!'

'He said, in Jyathaima's prayer room, behind the Kali picture (Herbert touched his forehead in respect), behind it is Binu's diary.'

Jyathaima struggled to rise from the mat: 'Here, help me up. Mother, my knees, oh mother mine.'

Herbert remembered it clearly, Jyathaima, hobbling in front, then Herbert, then Dhanna-dada and boudi, and finally Krishna-dada climbing up the badly lit stairs. Then, the door of the prayer room was unbolted. The dim light was switched on. The picture of Kali hanging almost in the middle of the wall. Jyathaima first bowed her head before the goddess, then gripped the lower edge of the picture and tugged. A lizard darted out from behind it, ran up across the wall. 'Dhanna, pull,' Jyathaima said, 'She's so heavy—how I can lift her alone?'

A large picture of Kali, set in a heavy frame.

They pulled at its lower edge, but nothing happened.

'If there was something, it should have fallen out by now.'

'Why don't the lot of you just bring her down?' Jyathaima said, 'Then see if there's anything behind her.'

They saw it, as soon as they brought her down and turned her around. Screwed to the wooden frame, covered in cobwebs and dust—a small diary.

'Peeyu kahaan!' screamed a toothless mouth downstairs, 'Peeyu kahaan!'

'Oh! So many, so many crows! Pecking and pecking the glass from this side, that side. Flapping and clapping their wings. And in the middle of all that, someone singing! Binu smiling nonstop. I couldn't hear a thing. Then, like a voice in an empty room . . . I heard him clearly . . . he spoke—and then he died again just like that other time.'

Herbert could sense it. He would have to charge-barrage now. Binu had had his time. It was Herbert's time now. He would have to produce panic-pandemonium. Rip apart everything, torment-turmoil everything until the entire universe whirled in the dance of devastation.

Once upon a time, this land was home to many sages who were spirit-knowledge masters. We have heard that, in the present time too, elsewhere in the world too, many spirit-knowledge masters have been born. But their opinions are different from those of our sages. According to our sages, when one has become a ghost, then that ghost may be called or attracted, and that even the ghosts of gods and goddesses may be so called or attracted . . . We have heard that the present-day spirit-knowledge masters can, or indeed do, summon any dead person; in fact,

one of them is rumored to have called the soul
of the Buddha, no less.

—*Mysteries of the Afterlife*

With a sputter in my chest and a flutter in my
breast, I drew closer to the window, I had but
risen from my bed a moment ago—when my
glance fell low upon the floor and I saw, to my
astonishment—five or seven freshly severed
human heads rolling about the room. Their monstrous mocking smiles—their furious frowning
eyebrows—their lick-lolling tongues aroused in
my heart a terror so extreme—I stood there,
frozen like a statue—not daring to take even a
single step more. The very next instant there
came another sky-splitting scream.

—'The Horribly Haunted Circus'

Peeyu kahaan! Peeyu kahaan!

*

Krishna-dada went back home, and Herbert told
Jyathaima that he'd be using the downstairs room for his
business.

Five

If you do not offer this supreme sacrifice
Our India shall never arise, never arise

—*Dwarakanath Gangopadhyay*

It was Dhanna who told the whole neighbourhood about Herbert's dream-discovery of Binu's diary. When Dhanna told them, sitting at the Corporation park one Sunday evening, Barilal, Khettra, Gobi, Unjey, Haratal and the other *seniors* were stunned.

Gobi, the alcoholic, turned his bloodshot eyes to the waters of the Corporation pond, and said pensively, 'Actually, you know what, it's all the Mother's doing. Who knows when she'll tap whose head with a divine finger. How else could our Herbert pull off such a miracle?'

'Many people say that, in Tarapith, there's a holy man's grave. If you pour a whole bottle of booze on it, you get visions of the future, see things.'

'No need to go so far. Go, just go to Ghutiari Sharif. Go and see what goes on there.'

'Must go see Herbert, once,' Barilal said, 'I'd like to hear it all for myself.'

Barilal's real reason for wanting to visit Herbert was different. His brother Gama had died last year, died of liver-rot caused by too much drinking. Died, dead, all right, but ever since then, today this one had fever, tomorrow that one had diarrhoea, day-after some other one failed an exam . . . Perhaps Herbert could offer a clue?

A few of the neighbourhood boys had been in Herbert's room, then.

By then, the steel of Herbert's resolve had acquired a new edge.

He stared, unblinking, at Barilal for a few moments. Then said: 'A year ago, no?'

'Yes, yes, eleven months. We did all the prayers and rest-in-peace rites, then. And soon, when it's a full year, we'll do them again.'

'All that's well and good, but the poor thing's dying without water.'

'Who?'

'Who else? The champa tree, my dear, the champa tree.'

The words struck a chill in Barilal's heart. The terrace garden had been Gama's only passion. And there, in a wooden box, he had planted a champa tree. That was true.

From his top-terrace, Herbert had often seen Gama tending the potted plants in the evenings, turning up their soil, watering them.

He had also seen, more recently, that blossoming champa tree drying to its death.

Barilal stood up, wanting to rush back home. And Herbert dealt his masterstroke.

'If you see it's dead, throw it away and plant a new one in the rains. If it lives, then no more to be said. Just a few days of watering, and you'll know one way or other.'

Barila's legs threatened to give way. But Herbert didn't stop, stopping was no longer an option, stopping was impossible.

'They don't go away, you know. The ties that bind. I'll die. I'll burn. But wherever the ties remain, therever I'll return. Wherelse can I go? Such are the Invisible games, the Indiscernible diversions. Such an abundance of arrangements. But—all that some other day. Now go home, Bari-da, and do as I told you.'

Barilal's tender mercies ensured that the champa tree revived, sprouted new leaves. Burst out in a babble of new branches.

Dhanna had shared the dream story with a handful of his friends. But Barilal tirelessly shared the plant story with as many people as he could until news of it travelled far and wide.

News of it even reached the Chief Inspector who couldn't believe his ears: 'Really? Just like Nostradamus! I should go see him for myself.'

Then one morning, perched on a rickshaw, Koton and Somnath brought back a sheet of wood-framed tin—red letters painted on a yellow background—a shiny new signboard: 'Conversations with the Dead. Prop: Herbert Sarkar.'

Before he took Binu's diary and went back home, Krishna-dada gave Herbert a hundred rupees. That was what Herbert used to start his business. Even Krishna-dada, despite his reluctance and deep opposition, had come to believe, been forced to believe, in Herbert's dream. To tell the truth, Herbert had completely forgotten that Binu had spoken those words to him in the hospital. When Binu died, when Binu was burning, all those policemen, policevans, policeguns—all that had scared the living daylights out of Herbert, wiped his memory clean.

*

A perusal of Mrinal Kanti Ghosh Bhakti-bhushan's *Accounts of the Afterlife* will result not only in strengthening one's belief in spiritualism and the existence of the soul but also in revealing ways in which one may speak with or even glimpse one's departed loved ones.

Judged from a *spiritualist* perspective, the techniques employed by Herbert for communicating and conversing with dead were, at best, a hodgepodge.

The technique of contacting dead souls by raps on the table, adopted by the Fox sisters of America and making them world famous, that technique of *rapping* cast no shadow over Herbert's dialogues with the dead.

The technique of invisible writing on a sheet of slate or paper rumoured to have been displayed by Eglinton-shaheb in 1881 in Calcutta, that too was never done— or rather, could not be done—by Herbert.

In one sense, perhaps one could call Herbert a sort of *medium*.

On this matter of *mediums*, Herbert had learnt from *Accounts of the Afterlife*:

Over and above these methods of conversing and communicating with the dead are others that require the presence of an intercessor. Such an intercessor is referred to in English as a *medium*. One cannot say for certain if all men possess the strength to be a medium. But that not all mediums possess the same strength— that has been proven beyond doubt. It has been observed that despite their lack of learning and letters, some persons are born with such ability or somehow attain it during their childhood years. Yet many others have, despite their every effort, proven futile at such attainment. There are those who believe that persons who are Libran by birth and peaceable by nature, persons who are strong enough to restrain their emotions, those are the persons best suited to be mediums. Or, in other words, they are the persons who may most easily be made to surrender to the will of the dead soul. Such are the reasons for the greater number of mediums being found among women.

Suddenly, in a dream, Herbert attaining the ability of communing with the hereafter—such instances are rare in the world of spiritualists.

Herbert had never tried the *planchette* technique. It could be said, however, that he had to some degree put to use the technique of *automatic writing*. Of course, if one compared the samples of his occasional and haphazard use of this technique with those in the collected volumes of William Stead's *Borderland* magazine (especially the writings by Miss Julia's spirit) or with those accomplished by W. Stainton Moses, then one would surely be reduced to laughter.

There were a few times when Herbert displayed the signs of being a *trance medium*. Although he never showed any signs of prophecy or *clairvoyance*. Nor could he ever become a *healing medium*. He did not possess the power to mesmerize. And the power to give form to the soul, to cause a *materialization*—that was beyond him entirely.

Richet, Crookes, Conan Doyle, Meyers—there should be no attempt to connect Herbert to the long line of this glorious tradition. He had no relation either with those in Calcutta who devoted themselves to the study of souls and free spirits, among whose number could be counted a living legend of the cultural world. Herbert was a *freak*.

And, of course, once his business began to thrive, his good sense left him entirely. There was nothing he wouldn't do for money. Sometimes, holding an object that belonged to the dead, or gazing at a scrap of their handwriting, he would pretend to analyse it through *psychometry*. Besides, it is practically common knowledge that true spiritualists don't approve of establishing contact with the hereafter in the middle of the afternoon, in the middle of the night, in the dead of winter or the height of summer, in rain or storm or thundershower, for at those times they are most likely to come across ghosts and ghouls. At those times, free spirits are almost entirely absent. But Herbert had no right time—wrong time. Herbert had no time, not even time to stop.

One of his first clients was Binayendra Chowdhury and his wife Atashi. Binayendra's only son had been a pilot. Who died in an Airbus accident in Hyderabad. About a year ago. They had been thinking of getting him married, Rahul, their son . . .

Since his death, Atashi had all but lost her mind . . .

Binayendra-babu smoked one cigarette after another. Atashi stared unblinkingly at Herbert. And Herbert, Herbert sat ramrod straight, staring unblinkingly at Rahul's photograph.

Then, after some time, he closed his eyes.

(Koton and the other boys had been sent outside.)

Then, after some more time, he opened his eyes, picked up a *dot pen* and scrawled M–4 on a sheet of paper. Then, with a gentle smile, he pushed the photograph back towards Binayendra-babu.

Then he began to speak:

'Untimely death. Meant to live long, work hard—but who knows why and how the thread snapped. Grief! Sorrow! Despair! And that's not all. Your deaths too! Oh, I don't know where you found such fortitude. I bow before you, I bow before such strength.'

Atashi burst out crying. Herbert stopped for a moment to wipe his own tears. Then smiled gently again.

'But there is no more need for sorrow. None at all. Time, death—these are part of life. I see the boy's mind was full of god.'

'Peeyu kahaan!' came a roar from the first floor, terrifying Binayendra and Atashi, 'Peeyu kahaan!'

'As far as I knew,' Binayendra said a moment later, 'Khoka had no time for religion.'

'None at all?'

'None. In fact, he was dead against it. The wife's a disciple of Sai Baba . . .'

'Stop!' screamed Herbert, clapping his hands over his ears, 'Stop! Say no more! I won't listen, no, no, no!'

Binayendra and Atashi were totally taken aback.

A moment later Herbert uncovered his ears and chuckled wryly. 'Forgive me. Never learnt my letters, so never learnt to hold my tongue. Now, just for a moment, let us assume you are correct. But if you are indeed correct, then how can this be so?'

'How can what be so?'

Herbert pointed to the paper, to the M–4 scrawled upon it.

'What does that mean?'

'Mean? If I tell you what it means, then my game is done. Oh, oh, oh, here come Shiva and Durga, such a plan being hatched, I tell you. Tell me, in this superslick-superficial age, how many can achieve even the middle level of virtue? How many can ascend to the fourth plane? When I die, do you think I'll get there? No, I'll be one of the lowest lapsees, slowly devoured by the poka-pests of hell. Your son, on the other hand, now lives in eternal joy—as if in the garden of the gods, as if in the body of a demigod, glowing with the light of divine bliss.'

Atashi, entranced, hangs upon his every word.

'And you know what he said? He said: "Puja-prayers, all that stuff's useless, you have to know how to die." He was full of good thoughts when he died, so he's reaping the rewards now. Such joy, such joy, Mother, Mother mine, why did you not show us all this earlier, Mother . . . why?'

A grave Binoyendra-babu led a silent Atashi into the back seat of their Ambassador car and went home, his heart full with the knowledge that his pilot son had attained the state of medium virtue, acquired abundant joy and ascended to the fourth plane—and his wallet lighter by the weight of two 50-rupee notes.

'Your . . .'

'My?'

'I mean, how much should I give?'

'Give? Give. Don't want to give? Don't give. He who lives on alms, he who is spat upon daily, how can he have a price? If I had at least a degree or two, then perhaps I could have told you how much you should give.'

On the way out, Binayendra tucked two 50s beneath Herbert's pillow.

That night itself, 20 was spent on a bottle and 80 put away in the trunk.

*

A few days later, Herbert climbed up to the first floor and gave his Jyathaima a hundred rupees and his Dhanna-boudi a box of sweets. 'For Phuchka and Bulan. A treat from their uncle.' Big-big sweets for their big-big blows. Didn't spare a kicking for Dhanna-dada either: 'Dada, I hope you tried the sweets?' Dhanna-dada had emitted only a grunt in reply.

A few more days later, Dhanna-boudi said, 'Thakurpo, so many maids and servants, all using that outside bathroom. Why don't you use the one inside the house instead? Has anyone told you not to?'

'Thank you, boudi, but I've gotten used to that one. Besides, my timings are all mixed up now. Really, it's no trouble at all.'

'Actually, it was your dada's idea, to ask you. I'm just passing it along.'

*

The one who was the happiest was Jyathaima. Placing a hand on Herbert's head, she said, 'How you've brought me joy, Haru. Such torment, such torture, don't think I didn't see a thing. I don't say a word, but I see everything, know everything. It's a sacred task you're performing, son, and it's all the goddess' doing.'

'Jyathaima!'

'Yes?'

'Tell me that story, no.'

'Which one?'

'The one about your wedding...'

'The sweet! Hee-hee-hee-hee! That was the night before our first night together. The new son-in-law was pecking at his food. If he picked up the luchi on one side, then the potato slid off the other. Almost asleep he was.'

'But why?'

'Because the friends who'd accompanied him, they'd secretly brought along some booze. He'd drink every day, he would. So many kinds of bottles . . . Anyway, then . . .'

'Then? Jyathaima—wake up! What then?'

'Then, by then all the women were giggling. Why? They'd given the new son-in-law a sweet, a sweet as big as an elephant's head!'

'Then?'

'By then your Uncle was rimful-brimful. But yes, as strong as Balaram. So he bit into it. But as soon as he bit—as soon as he . . . oh dear, what a terrible to-do . . . hee-hee-hee-hee . . .'

'But why, Jyathaima?'

'Because inside the sweet was a shoe! A whole shoe! One of a pair! He put the shoe down on the plate. Began to look around him with those big-big eyes. And the women, all the women shouting: "The groom's eating a shoe! Oh dear, what do we do?" Ah, it was such a fabulous joke!'

Did Girishkumar suddenly recall the memory of that night? Is that why he screamed just then, 'Peeyu kahaan! Peeyu kahaan!'

'Oof, that peeyu kahaan, peeyu kahaan! When Dhanna–Krishna were little boys, when they'd been bad boys, he'd swear at them. "Sons of bitches!" And they'd mutter under their breaths, "Your loins' riches." All a memory now. Such authority, such personality. All sucked up by that peeyu kahaan, peeyu kahaan . . . Oh Haru, I've remembered a song. Shall I sing it for you?'

'Oh please do. You sing so well.'

'Listen, then. But can I catch the tune again?'

'Yes. Yes, of course you can.'

By the light of the moon, Jyathaima began to sing:

Sister
How to the Yamuna do I dare?
On the way to the water   lo, the beauty I beheld
Such beauty is surely beyond compare.

Like a dark cloud full of rain,   is he, an enchanting sight
Listen, listen, oh sister of my heart.
My heart no more my own remains   the heart I lost, 'twas he who gained
To whom dare I this shame-truth impart?

A meek and modest maid am I   but his splendour when I spy
I feel my thoughts and senses go astray
The water pot gapes with barren brim   As I gaze and gaze and gaze at him
Tell me, sister, can I go on this way?

When I hear him play the flute   I rush from my room down the river route
Oh but of a calamity I should beware.
My husband's mother, his sisters dear   will shame and scold me I do fear
How to the Yamuna do I dare?

The song trails off. And Jyathaima heaves and heaves
with sobs. A slant-sliver of moonlight falls upon a cupboard door and spatters everything with silver. Mingled
with the light from Dhanna's television, it paints the
veranda with a blazing blue glow. As he walks away from
his aunt who sits still in that light, Herbert sees his uncle

leaning against the wall and staring with deep tenderness at his wife.

Herbert cried all the way back to his room.

Back in his room, Herbert's heart ached. The top-terrace, the shadows, the night, the morning, the crow's call—his heart ached for them all. His heart ached for his father. His heart ached for his mother. His heart ached for his uncle. His heart ached for his aunt. Everything and everywhere, a tie that bound, a string that pulled. His heart ached for every one.

Back in his room, Herbert how-howled into his pillow. Cried for Binu. Cried for himself. Cried for Buki. Cried for all the lies he'd told. Cried and cried until he fell asleep. Then cried in his sleep. Then turned over in his sleep. Then laughed in his sleep. Then cried. Then laughed.

Father Lalitkumar and mother Shobharani had been observing their child and his rather extraordinary exertions. An astonished Lalitkumar looked enquiringly at his wife, who said, with an enigmatic smile, 'Just dream-delighting with the gods.'

*

Herbert's business began to thrive. A doctor came, with his brother's wife. The brother had died in America, died of cancer. An air-hostess came. She wanted to speak to her father. A medium-built boy came one day. For his mother. Couldn't have been older than First Year college. But he was not impressed: 'Whatever you've told me, it's all *vague*. Not one *concrete* word. My mistake—I shouldn't have come.'

After he'd left, Herbert sat in silence for a few long minutes.

Then, 'Shouldn't have come!' he spat, 'Father's sister-fucking son! Did I tell you to come?'

Six

I'm lost without trace, oh won't you lift your face
That I may kiss you once, and once again

—*Swarajkumari Devi*

An evening in the winter of 1991, just like the evenings of three or four winters past. Herbert put on his Ulster overcoat and the pants from Binu—dead 20 years now—looked at himself in the mirror, and was at once utterly charmed by his own reflection.

'*Cat, bat, water, dog, fish!*' he whispered.

What will Herbert do now? Of the adventure he was about to embark upon, he had only a vague idea. A 20-minute walk would take him to the shaheb neighbourhood—just the sound of the street names gave him such a thrill—Loudon, Rawdon, Robinson, Short, Outram, Wood, Park . . .

Their successive sightings of such a curiouser character may have led the ayahs and durwans to think he was a mad man. At the same time, a closer look may have led them to think that in his veins must be flowing the blood of a white man. Or else how to explain that fair skin, that blueish-eyed gaze . . .

Herbert is walking. Suddenly, in front of a *packers and movers*, he stops. Is he about to say something? There was something he wanted to say. Never mind, it can wait.

Herbert walks on. 'Cat, *bat, water, dog, fish!*' Herbert mutters under his breath

Smells waft out of the cake shop. The cake shop, its windows of tinted glass. Will he go in? Oh god, how large that house is. How enormous the gate. A Maruti is reversing up the driveway, its tail lights flashing white. The homeowners in the car—Herbert knows the house far better than they. There must be a wooden staircase inside. Leading up to a point, and then splitting into a right and a left. Where it splits, there hangs a mirror encased in a black wooden frame which rests on a *stand* whose round-round feet are shaped like tiger paws. On either side of the mirror towers a tall brass vase.

Herbert was used to climbing the stairway on the right. But—what were the rooms like upstairs, how many rooms were there, what had happened in those rooms, who lived in them?

Herbert's head hurts. He lights a cigarette.

An old iron water trough, once meant for the horses, sits along on the side of the pavement. Herbert perches on its rim. '*Cat, bat, water, dog, fish!*' he mutters under his breath.

Yet he can see, shadowy and unclear, dressed in white, so flimsy-fine, the skin so fair, so gold the hair . . . Herbert shuts his eyes and keeps on seeing . . . A candle, glowing, someone coming closer, someone leaning towards it to blow out its flame . . . the sound of glasses clinking . . .

Herbert opens his eyes. It is dark. The streetlamps are dark too. Only the cars glowing by.

Herbert thought two thoughts at once: that he had something to say, and that this house did not have that top-terrace.

*

A famous jeweller's son had come to him, accompanied by his employees, but Herbert's words had deeply embarrassed him. Made his face flush red.

'What nonsense! My father was like a god. Ask these men, they all worked with him for years—Mr Das, tell him—'

'What have I said that I need to ask them? What have I said that's so hard to swallow? That's sticking in your throat? Have I called him names?'

'Yes, you did—you called him a sinner.'

Herbert burst out laughing. 'Only a minor sinner, I said. Only a third-plane dweller. Do you know what that means that you've started yack-quacking?'

The young man falls silent. The young man sits still and listens. 'A businessman, he was. So he's cast a huge big net, then he's drawing it in, now the fish are scrabbling, now he's grabbing the males from this pond and chucking them into that—what, understood?'

'But, sir, we have no fish . . . we're in the jewellery . . .'

'Oh-ho, these are all riddles, don't you see? You must solve them. When I say businessman, I mean a man of possessions and property, a man of plots and plans, a man taking a bit of time to get over the death-shock. At the very most, I give him a year and a half . . . then he'll be free. Zoom about in glee. Oh, such are these mysterious ways!'

'So, what should we do now?'

'You? Nothing. Focus on the business. But yes, he has that worry about the land.'

'Land?'

'Yes, yes, land. Says he's very concerned, very unhappy. Is there something fishy about it?'

'Well, there's that bit of land in Barasat, there's a court case on . . .'

'No, no, I don't need to know. Settle it if you can. I don't care.'

'We should go now. Your fee . . . ?'

'Here, you can keep it right here. What's it to you— just my sins that're gathering interest. All right, gentlemen. May the goddess go with you.'

There was another man waiting outside. Long hair. Glasses. Quite *smart*. Wearing a *raw-silk bush shirt* the colour of clotted cream and *full pants* the colour of *chocolate*. As soon as the jewellers left, he stepped into the room. 'When are you free to talk?'

'Please, go ahead. I'm free right now.'

'No, not now. I don't have time right now. Got a taxi waiting. You take cases in the evenings?'

'I'm sorry, no. I go out in the evenings.'

'Go out? Well, staying in one evening won't hurt you. This is *important*.'

Herbert feels a twinge of anxiety. 'Am I in some kind of jam?'

'Jam? Well, from one point of view it's a bit of jam I suppose. *Heavy* sticky jam. All right, I'll come when it's time. When are you back?'

'I'm usually home by 7.30.'

'Yes, of course you are. So that you can drink with the local lumpen. See, I know everything. All right, I'm off. Goodbye.'

'But why don't you just speak plainly? This sounds highly suspicious.'

'Let it. I'll be back. Sweep the suspicions away. Goodbye.'

*

A car was driving out of the Robinson Street *nursing home*. Its driver wore a white peaked cap. Inside sat a *lady doctor*, *bob-haired* and beautiful, the sight of whom rendered Herbert speechless-stunned. A foreign car. A Toyota or a Datsun, something like that. Those cars have such great *suspension* that you can hardly tell they're moving, they just roll away from you like a wave. And as one such wave flowed past him, the *lady doctor* tossed her head and shook a strand of hair off her face that Herbert saw and that statue-froze him to the spot, mouth hanging open in astonishment. Through the glass he saw that face. That old familiar face. He had something terribly important to say. But the *lady doctor* didn't stop to listen. The driver drove on. The *lady doctor* went away.

Who was it who climbed up that wooden staircase?

Herbert was coming down the wooden stairs on the right of the framed mirror, and on the left the one who was going up, the one whose back, *bobbed hair*, shoulders, waist, white clothes, frills on those white clothes . . . The *lady doctor's* profile glimpsed through the car window in the winter of 1991 was for Herbert an extraordinary encounter, *lady doctor*, wait, please, don't go away like that. I don't have breath enough to run after your car, I'll never catch up with your car—wait, listen—what harm can it do to just listen, if only I could stand in front of the mirror again and if only I could remember again—oh . . .

Herbert's head hurts. The Ulster swarm-warms around him. Big-big buttons. As he wrenches them open, one, like a big black medal, comes off and flies from his fingers. Herbert gropes on the ground for it. Picks it up. Puts it in his pocket.

What did Herbert want to tell the *lady doctor*?

Herbert walks on. 'Cat, bat, water, dog, fish!' Herbert mutters under his breath.

When he went out in the evenings, evening after evening, he spent hours waiting outside the *nursing home* but never saw the *lady doctor* again. He was angry. Hurt. But who gave a damn? The *lady doctor* had gone away. Didn't stop to listen to no one.

Herbert walks on. Makes a sound with his mouth like a machine-gun. Herbert had seen a machine-gun. In a movie.

Ratatatatat.

*

A half-mad man stumbled in. His sister had run away. A few months later, after identifying fillets of her flesh in a found trunk at Howrah Station, he had lost his mind. So he had come to Herbert.

'Can't bear the sight of *trunks*, *suitcases*, closed boxes of any kind. Keep seeing her hair hanging out from under the lid. I'll open the lid, and then I'll see—'

The man's clothes were unwashed and untidy. Bursting into tears, he shook his head and pleaded, 'Can't. Can't *stand* it any more. Please *help* me. Or I *shall die*. I beg you, please help me. You can, you can *communicate* with the *dead* . . . my sister . . .'

His sobs grew louder, swelled into wails. He cried for a long time. Then he took out a grubby handkerchief and wiped his face, rubbed his glasses.

'What was her name?'

'Shanta.'

Santa—Herbert wrote on a piece of paper. Then drew a line under it.

'Got a photo or something?'

'No. But after she'd run away, a letter had come. I've got a Xerox. Will that do?'

'Why a Xerox?'

'The *original*'s at police headquarters, in Lalbazar.'

'Oh oh! Police! Lovely time you're having, aren't you? All right, I don't need to read it. Just to touch it. But you have to be patient, sit for a while. In fact, why don't you go out for a bit? These things tend to work better when I'm on my own.'

'All right, I'll come back later. But please, you have to help me. I'm telling you I'll go mad otherwise.'

Herbert had no idea what to say. Closing the door behind him, he grabbed Accounts of the Afterlife and, by the light streaming in through the window, frantically scrabbled through its pages. Hoping to patch something together from 'Dead Sister Brought Back by Brother's Devotion': 'It was in 1872. The chief employee of Jessore's Chanchraraj Sarkar, the (now) late Nabinchandra Basu, was then in residence with his family at No. 3 Sookia Street . . . had she become a ghost then?' But no, there was nothing there. Nor in 'Revenge of the Wasted Wife' nor in 'Haunting the Husband's Harlot.' 'My Departed Daughter Jyotsna' provided the gem that the higher a soul ascended, the brighter it tended to glow. Yes, but so what? Herbert was growing more and more tense, more and more scared. About all of it. What the hell kind of case was this anyway?

Suddenly, someone knocked on the door.

With a quaking heart, Herbert opened it—but it was only Pachu, from the tea shop, come to collect the glasses. And he said no, there was no one waiting at the shop, no one waiting to come back here. Sliding his feet into his sandals, Herbert followed Pachu out, walked over to the cigarette shop, walked over to the bus stop, walked everywhere. Looked everywhere. That man was gone.

That man never came back.

The copy of Shanta's letter stayed behind with Herbert, was left behind in his pile of papers, all with addresses scribbled on them.

But the things he could have told the man—those turned out to be useful. A young doctor, a child *specialist*, had brought to Herbert the beautiful Belgian actress Tina. It was Tina's first visit to India. She was a TV and a stage actress. A crowd had gathered outside Herbert's door in the hope of catching a glimpse of her. The doctor was acting as interpreter, translating Herbert's words into English for her. Tina's mother had also been an actress. But a car accident had crippled her. Tina's father married again. Tina's mother was now dead. Tina was very sad. Herbert was only too familiar with the actions and accomplishments of dearly beloved motherly souls—Tina being a foreigner, he had also deployed, with flawless aim, some *basic theory*—the afterlife comprised six sorts of spirits—what each was like—who inhabited which plane—how a mother's love acted like a shield around her children. Tina said, she'd visited a Tibetan lama in London. He had also told her about the six-spirit system, but had not been able to tell her where her mother was nor how she was.

The memshaheb paid a hundred rupees to Herbert. Herbert's reputation multiplied a thousandfold. The doctor made sure Herbert signed a receipt.

'You're on a roll, boss! When's the mem-femme coming again?'

'As soon as she needs to. I gave her quite a *dose*.'

'Boss, did you really close the door and show her a ghost in private?'

'You lot are so full of shit, I tell you. Know this, that Herbert doesn't sniff at every hole for honey. Mem-femme! Hah, I've seen hundreds!'

*

Although he never saw the *lady doctor* again, through the glass window of a closed antique store on Park Street, Herbert did see the fairy. And at once he realized that of the *lady doctor*, of the woman who climbed up the wooden stairs on the left of the mirror, this fairy was the younger version. Buki had been a little older than the fairy. But the Buki he'd gazed at from his top-terrace, that Buki had been different. He couldn't match the two and come up with the one. But the fairy was the beginning.

Golden hair, carved out of a yellowish stone. A stone body, draped in stone robes. The left hand gently folded behind her head. The right arm holding aloft a lamp. The light must come on at the touch of a switch, for a black electric wire trails away behind her. The sight of that wire upsets Herbert, makes him uncomfortable. And all those things, so many things, around her! Stone vases, stone chairs, wooden elephants whose faces were turned away, a stone table on which was placed an enormous lamp from some enormous ship.

'*Cat, bat, water, dog, fish!*'

As Herbert stared at the fairy, he thought he heard the dead women of the West singing their songs. Swelling into a cloud of lament, the songs drew closer and hurled themselves against the dusty glass. Alas, stone fairy. Like that young Russian woman facing the German machine-guns—naked, her hands hiding her breasts, running across the dark black ground. Not stopping to listen to anyone. If the busy pedestrians stopped for a moment, they would hear the entranced Herbert's stifled sobs. And see that fairy slowly floating upwards, her cheeks rubbing against a bulbous big balloon tied to a ladder with string.

On winter's Park Street, a streak of *refrigerator* air sidled up and clasped Herbert in its arms. Herbert turned up the collar of his Ulster, and now it was impossible to look at him and think of anything but Hollywood. It was still evening, now. It had still been evening, then. Soon, when darkness spreads, the fairy will seep away from view. Only to be sometimes startled by the lights of a passing car. Then, her lips will seem to move. Then, her blind eyes will seem to gleam with yellow light. 'Staystill, staysafe,' whispered Herbert, 'I'll be back.'

On the way home, to the trees by the street, to the familiar lepers, to the balcony pillars, to the signboards and tea shop, to the duty-done homeward-bound ayahs and nurses, to the prostitutes, park railings and the pictures of a lion and a Mickey Mouse painted on the walls of the park pond, to the water spurting out of the depths of the city—to each and every one he had something special-specific to say. Car lights splayed across the giant hoardings, and Herbert felt he was at the movies again. Standing in the heart of a crowd, in the middle of some street, Herbert and Krishna-dada had watched *Fall of Berlin*. And many other documentaries about the Second World War. A naked young Russian woman hides her breasts with her hands and runs across the dark black ground while the German soldiers slowly raise their machine-guns. The woman runs, runs on and on. Not stopping to listen to anyone.

Ratatatatat.

*

The wheel of time spun round and round. 1992 arrived, armed with a litany of shame and blame, calumny and corruption, thievery and treachery. But Herbert's year began well enough. A Bengali newspaper or two published the odd article or two. Nothing much in January. Nothing much in February—no, there were a few cases, off and on. Then again nothing much in March. Herbert was happy enough with whatever money he was making. But not with the smoking-drinking expenditure which had risen dramatically. Herbert decided that since Dol was on 18 March, he'd carry on with his flamboyant spending until then. From the day after, he'd leave-let go of everything, lead a fully frugal-*type* of life. Herbert was slowly running out of swagger too. The machine was giving trouble—sound, yes, but picture, no. Sometimes picture, yes, but sound, no. Man was a TV, after all. For a few days now, different parts of Herbert's body had been emitting different croaks and creaks.

'Tell me, dear,' Jyathaima said, 'You seem to be making good enough money. Then why is that body of yours as thin as fish bone? Must be too much drink.'

'No, no, nonsense, Jyathaima. Actually, it's hard work, very hard work. Bone-crushingly hard. That's why all my marrow-fat's drying up—it's not getting a chance to stay in my bones.'

'Oh but that's a sign of sainthood! What good will it do to my Haru to be like that? I'm going to find you a girl, get you married. Tie you down a little.'

'Who do you think will want to marry me?'

'Who won't? And why won't they? An earning boy. A god-looking boy. So many girls just waiting. You roll the beads. Then see how they come, chasing them home.'

The beads roll, roll away. No one chases after them, no one follows them home to Herbert. Not Buki. Not the *lady doctor*. And the fairy? No, Herbert simply cannot bring himself to imagine the stone fairy as his bride.

*

Dol was a riot of colours. Someone put something peculiar in Herbert's hair—the more he washed it, the more it gave out colour.

The day after Dol. Still hungover. When bang in the middle of the afternoon, the doors to Herbert's room were flung open by that sisterfucker who'd come that one time wearing a *raw-silk bush shirt* the colour of clotted cream and who'd left promising to turn up again and sweep his suspicions away. Herbert was deep-dreaming then, that he was in a hospital hallway lined with big glass jars containing bits and pieces of the human body, aborted foetuses without eyes or mouths, that he was running through that hallway, that he was running and that a naked woman was running with him. But how will he get out with a woman who's wearing no clothes? Wait, there was a way. In the hospital grounds, in the shady-shadowy spots, some hookers hawked dead women's things. Herbert bought a cheap *nylon* saree for the naked woman. She put it on, and then they came out from the hospital gates and found themselves in front of the tram depot. But instead of boarding a tram, they climbed into a rickshaw. The rickshaw lurched on its way. Suddenly, Herbert looked down and was got the shock of his life—how had he not noticed that the woman had *high heels* on! Her armpit, there, just beside him. And just beside that her nylon-saree-covered breasts . . .

Herbert's eyes snapped open.

And saw clotted-cream *bush shirt* leaning over his face.

'Sleeping, eh? Then how will I sweep your suspicions away?'

Herbert jolted up in bed.

'Didn't I tell you, I'd come back when it's time? Arise, awake, O Herbert the Great. For I am about to change your fate.'

The man opened his briefcase and took out a flat bottle of booze. Took out two fragile-fine glasses. A pack of Classic cigarettes. A lighter.

'Go, you witless wanker, go take a piss and then come back here and squat tight. Don't stare at me like a disobedient donkey. Do just as I say. And you'll jack off the jackpot, and I'll be Chengiz Khan.'

Thumping-hearted Herbert thud-scudded off to pee. By the time he got back, the man was ready with two poured-full drinks. Each took a glass, lit a cigarette. 'Not cheers,' the man said, 'not skol. We're Bengali, and everyone in Bengal now says: Joy!'

'Joy!' Herbert repeated.

The man's name was Surapati Marik. Plots and property, fish farms, coal mines, mopeds—a broker for a wide variety of goods and services, he'd amassed an immense expanse of experience. Those who started computerized horoscopes in India—Mr Marik has been in on that too. Now, dead-desperate to start big-league *professional football* in India. Russi Mody, Ratan Tata, Chhabria, Ambani—he'd spent the last three years talking football to them all. But now, right now, he had Herbert in his sights. Now, casting a loving look at Herbert, he said, 'Look, my boy, I don't believe a word of all that ghost-toast stuff. Don't believe you're hugger-mugger with the lot of them, don't disbelieve either. I just know one thing—a tilapiya in a tank will never grow to full size.'

'Meaning, dear sir, that I'm a tank-trapped tilapiya?'

'Or what? Carp in a lake or whale in the ocean? I believe in calling a *spade* a *spade*.'

'Then why don't you get to the point? Cough it up, whatever you're on about. Or I'll soon be too sloshed to care.'

Surapati Marik closes his eyes. '*Good, good,*' he says, 'All that petty-prattle I also *do not like*. The point is this— I am going take you to the *top level*. Take myself with you too. Or I wouldn't have got you this whisky for free. Whatever else you think, don't think me a fool. I've thrown heaps and handfuls of Herberts into the water. Then reeled them in again.'

Surapati Marik opens his eyes. 'A gleaming glass office,' he continues, 'AC-cool and classy. Pictures on the walls. A girl at a computer. The shelves shining with rows of pricey books on the subject. Music playing, softly-softly. Dim lights. Carpets. Five hundred rupees a visit. *Minimum. Special cases,* much more. Then Bombay, then Delhi. What message a dead *politician* is sending— to whisper it just once into the ears of a live one. And thus to capture a few *kingpins* and *big bulls*. Alongside: detachment, indifference. Then Dubai. Bahrain. Dead sheikhs, live sheikhs. Air India. Tata Sierra. RSVP. RIP . . . Oh, I can't go on. Hang on, let me pour another. This stuff's *smooth*, but. No?'

Herbert tried to pluck some courage from his swiftly soaring high, but somewhere inside him lurked a can't-do-it, just-can't-do-it feeling. 'Can't do anything without English. That's where they've all beat me to it.'

'English will get you fuck-all. You'll have an interpreter, you idiot—you'll speak, he'll satin-smooth translate. Any client gets hitchy-twitchy, he'll clench his teeth and call them names: *Fuck you! Tit! Cunt! Prick!*'

'So you think this will work? That I can make it work? I'm just scared I'll screw it all up.'

'Rubbish. You're too scareful for your own good. I, on the other hand—I'm carefree, scarefree. It'll be my set-up, after all. Fifty-fifty. Marik–Sarkar Enterprise.'

A pint in the tummy
Makes the bait seem very yummy . . .
And Herbert agrees, am I right?

'So, dear sir, when will you be back?'

'Aha. When I'll come, which day, what time—that's my business. *Marik alone will decide.* My mission is now to hold you aloft. Spread your scent from nose to nose. Washing powder Nirma!'

'Eh?'

'This bastard's a *spastic*, I tell you. Those kids who call you Titbirde, Titbird—I *support them.* Now, my No. 1 task is to organize some *publicity* for you. Tong-prong strategy.

On one side, a *whisper campaign* . . . hush-hush, low-buzz. On the other side, a couple of articles thrown into the English papers. Now, our collaboration has commenced. And I'm off. Oh, yes, you can keep the cigarettes. But you'd better stop ruining your liver drinking with those lout-lumpen-local-loafers. From now on, it'll be you and me, AC rooms and *dim* lights, and only Black Dog.'

Surapati Marik pinched Herbert's cheeks. 'Coochy coochy coochy coochy,' he cooed.

And left.

*

Evening thickens into night. In the dark, Herbert lights a Classic cigarette. Buki, *lady doctor*, fairy . . . the sadness will always swell, and yet, on the other side, little by little, the gates of heaven are opening.

In the dark, Herbert sings softly to himself:

> *Cat, bat, water, dog, fish . . .*
> *Cat, bat, water, dog, fish . . .*
> *Cat, bat, water, dog, fish . . .*
> *Cat, bat, water, dog, fish . . .*

The smoke from his cigarette draws pictures in the dark, even though no one can see.

The fire at its tip merely blows big, glows small.

Seven

Oh listen to the chorus   say, that this land
Is no land for lamentation.

—Hironmoyee Devi

April is the cruellest month, when clusters of virulent viruses run riot through the streets of Calcutta.

Street-dwellers and slum-dwellers had waged heroic wars against these viruses and somehow succeeded, through stubborn skullduggery, to develop resistant *antibodies*, or else so many of them wouldn't have lived to die under the slab of the *Stoneman*—the viruses would have wiped them out already, every he and she and family tree.

Unlike them, these mysterious and monstrous virus vampires have no trouble slaying flat the middle classes who, during the change-of-season, inevitably suffer from a lack of Vitamin C. Those adolescent girls whose thoughts of spring revelry, of blissful grazes against macho manes and manly fuzz, set their tender-tendril bodies aflame with acid desire—in the middle of their dirty dreams, they cry out 'oh yes, oh yes' to these viruses and then wake up from their siestas engulfed in phlegm.

And the adolescent boys: no sooner than they awaken—hardly opening their eyes—than they're choking in the viral wrestler's spiral armpit-hold.

It was just such a viral clusterfuck that found Herbert a sitting duck. As everyone knows, usually it is the higher-ups who hog the eggs hatched by the indefatigable fucking of the ducks. In this case, however, it's the doctors who relish them. For the virus-warfare weapons are entirely and only in their control.

It started with an ache in his back and waist and shoulder, and a streaming nose. He'd thought a plateful of deep-fried chilli-fat balls and a concentrated dose of local liquor ('Returning the empty bottles in unbroken condition will result in a Rs 2.05 refund per bottle') would force the fidge-fidge-nanny of a fever to flee his veins—but the *result* was the opposite. The fever reared its ugly head and roared. Scorched his senses. Made him vomit. Two days later, when Jyathaima found him unconscious, she shouted for Dhanna-dada. Dhanna rumble-grumbled his way to Dr Shetal, the homeopath in his chamber beside the *saloon*. Although the outcome of that visit was not very clear. Because the fever soared higher. Made him delirious.

'Got a brick! Got a brick!' he'd scream, and then fall back unconscious again. The fever took him far away. Somewhere else. He was stuck there. He didn't know where. At a dead end. Full of filth. The ground slippery and wet. But he couldn't turn back. Couldn't get out. Because on the trash mountain sat a one-eyed mangy cat. Waiting to pounce if he dared move an inch. So Herbert picked up a bit of brick, mustering up courage to throw it at the cat in case he twitched. And screamed: 'Just you try and bite me, you mangy cat you, I've got a brick. Got a brick.'

The doctor and Somnath silently exchange glances. Koka puts a cold compress on his forehead. So good that feels. Upstairs, up the wooden stairs, up in a room somewhere, the one who had drawn nearer, leant closer to blow out the candle, that someone was leaning over him now, looking into his eyes but his eyes cannot see . . . and the one-eyed mangy cat pounces . . .

'Got a brick! Brick! Bri . . .'

Once, he opened his eyes. Saw the room from deep underwater. Jyathaima, Somnath, Bulan, Koka . . . window . . .

'Jyathaima! Jyathaima!'

'Yes, dear. I'm right here.'

'So weak.'

'It's the fever, son. You'll be better soon.'

'That mangy cat keeps trying to bite me.'

'It won't come any more. I'll shoo it away.'

'Won't come?'

'No, it won't come.'

The mangy cat didn't come any more. But that night across Herbert's eyes came screaming and lurching a crowd of people of whom only the lower halves remained. Nothing but air above their legs. Somnath was dozing in a chair by his side. Herbert's whimpers woke him up and he quickly switched on a light. Herbert's eyes were shunting-hunting left and right and up and down. Then a little later he broke out in a sweat. Then fell asleep. Then Somnath fell asleep too.

For the rest of that night, only Shobharani stayed awake, cooling and caressing Herbert's forehead.

Oh, how soothing the scent of foreign *eau de cologne*.

The next day, they sent for Dr Sudhir. If he came home, it was 20 rupees a *visit*. He spent a long time examining Herbert. Then: 'Beastly form of *dengue*,' he concluded, 'the air's full of it these days. *Obscure viral origin*. It'll go, but it'll take *time*. I'm giving an *antibiotic capsule*. Three times a day for at least ten days. And a *vitamin*. Or he'll grow more weak. Light food. *Maximum rest*.'

'When can he have rice again, Doctor-babu?' asked Dhanna.

'He can have it right now. Just make a *paste* and give it to him. And any *light* food ... *soup* ...'

It was another week before Herbert felt a little better. Still slept most of the day, his cheeks and chin dark with stubble. The medicines, the special fish, the citrus fruits—Jyathaima paid for it all. Herbert's trunk hadn't been touched.

When Herbert was lying unconscious, then one day Surapati Marik had come. To let him know that he had made some progress. He talked to the boys and got all the details of Herbert's illness. Expressed relief that a good doctor was in place. Told them: 'Never mind. When he's a bit better, tell him absolutely no need to worry. Everything is proceeding according to plan. There should be two English pieces on him out soon. I'm off to the South for a few days. In case they come out when I'm gone, tell him I'll come back and then visit him with the *cuttings*. You fellows have done a lot. It's hard to see things like this, these days. This whole community thing is almost gone from the city. So nice to hear that's not true. Don't forget to tell him, please. Goodnight. Goodnight.'

He'd treated them all to Classic cigarettes. And his words had not been fake-faltu either. For, indeed, the second-last Saturday of April and the Sunday the week after, two separate English newspapers published two separate articles. 'Dead Speaks in the Divine Super-market' and 'Messages from the Other Side.'

The right people did not fail to notice the write-ups.

And the offices of both the newspapers were flooded with letters from the United States—from journals such as *Fate* and *Zetetic Scholar*—and from England—from *Fortean Times* and *Unexplained*—all making enquiries about Herbert.

Herbert spent all his days in sleep, undreaming unbroken sleep. Should he wake up and feel like reading, the doctor had left for him a copy of Kanti P. Dutta's *Gopal Bhaar at the Spooks' Soiree*. But he'd read only a few lines. And fall asleep again. And wake up again and see the half-dead evening light smeared upon the closed windowpane. The darkening room grows darker still. From a house down the lane, a song from a radio wafts and wanes. The shalik birds return to their cornice-cranny nests. Someone comes and switches on the light. And he falls asleep again. And wakes up again, and sees three or four of the boys sitting silently by his side.

'No more money coming in, boys. What the fuck fever is this! Bone and blood, it's sucking everything dry.'

'Just a few days more, Herbert-da, and you'll be tagra-tough again. And we're always here for you anyway.'

'Herbert-da, we were wondering . . . first say you won't get angry?'

Herbert knew what they were wondering. So he said, 'Just open the trunk and take some, no. But don't you dare give any to the lawyer's son.'

'No, no, boss. We'll just take 20 for us.'

'Twenty, twenty-five, take whatever you need. Oh, I feel so cold!'

'Wait, we'll pull your sheet up for you.'

'And one of you will stay here?'

'But of course, boss. Only one of us is going, getting and coming.'

'Going and coming. That's better, yes. That's good. Going and coming . . . going . . . and . . .'

Herbert fell asleep again.

Those who are masters of astrology, they con-
tend that every man is born with a record of his
responsibilities and duties in that life and a
detailed description of the consequences that
await him due to his actions in the last. A list
drawn up according to their past-performed
deeds and doings, a list drawn up by the hand
of God or the fingers of Fate. And who may say
what that list holds?

—*Mysteries of the Afterlife*

The sleeping Herbert is a sleeping beauty. Even when he sank into deep sleep waters, across those watery skies the sun still rose, the moon still shone. The stars opened wide their eyes and sent their light from a million light years away. Where even those who had no eyes felt its warmth upon them and startled-shook with pleasure.

Just as man is one kind, with many subordinate kinds, so too are ghosts one kind, with many subordinate kinds. Moreover, it would be erroneous to assume that all ghost kinds are comparable by disposition or by comportment. Among them too is displayed a great specificity of difference and distinction. Among them too may be observed variations such as wise ghost and foolish ghost, tranquil ghost and turbulent ghost, as the masters and maestros of spirit knowledge know only too well.

—*Op. cit.*

The ship lights shine bright. The turned-away wooden elephant turns around and swings his trunk. The one-eyed mangy cat tries to come in but flees at a nudge from the elephant's foot. Gopal had a molakat-meeting with a mamdo-mussalman ghost. Herbert lick-licks clear the stick of coloured glass candy. ' "Who are you?" asked Gopal, shivering in his shoes. "A mamdo!" came the instant reply.' The marble table, the marble chair, they swirl and twirl up in the air. The fairy like a butterfly flutters about the room of glass. Herbert kept start-starting awake. May Day, 1992. In Russia, Boris Yeltsin had organized a sensational soiree of ghosts.

Lakh-lakh Communists were confronted with the spirit of Capitalism. Rasputin was coming back, disguised as Solzhenitsyn. Yugoslavia was crumbling. Croatian tennis player Goran Ivanisevic was dreaming of a deadly serve that would wipe out Jim Courier and Andre Agassi. For the last time, the Commonwealth of Independent States—the Soviet Union—was preparing to go off for the games in Sweden. United Germany was confused about whom to include in its team—East? Or West? A man called Harshad Mehta was sitting in Bombay, waiting for a phone call from Delhi, waiting for permission to proceed with his plans. Poland, Czechoslovakia, Bulgaria, Romania, Albania—all engulfed in hubbub, hullabaloo. Communism was close to collapse . . . It was at just such a time that, in Calcutta, Herbert heard the rallying cries of May Day 1992 and thought for a moment that riots had broken out or that the country was finally free or that the 13 horsemen had come so easily and effortlessly . . .

On 16 May, feeling much better, Herbert climbed up to his top-terrace but later when evening fell he was overcome with exhaustion and slid into a stupor. By then, Saptarshi the Great Bear, Mrigashira the Orion, *quasars, pulsars, black holes, white dwarfs, red giants*— each and every sodding one had gathered in the sky. When a sliver of sense returned, Herbert saw that he was kneeling before ten enormous toenails growing out of someone's two enormous feet, someone's legs as high as the second floor, someone's colossal penis hanging higher, someone's swing-swaying testicles, someone's *jumbo* curls of pubic hair that were so much higher in the sky that they were barely visible, hazy-hazy to the eye.

Then that someone spoke to him, in a voice loud and deep enough to split the sky in two: 'Ha, ha, Herbert! Fruit of Lalitkumar's sperm and Shobharani's womb, scoundrel, damned despicable sisterfucker Herbert, bow low, bow low.'

'Who are you?'

'Son of a bitch! Who am I? I am Dhui.'

'You are Dhui! You?'

'Quiet! One more word and I'll kick your mouth shut. Look, there's my father Lambodar. That's not a cloud, that's him, my father. And there, see, Nishapati. And behind him, the one that's yelling, that's Sridhar.'

'Please—why is he yelling?'

'Karmic kickback has given him *fistulas* for ever. Should he be singing instead? No matter. You're doing well, you little shit, kicking goal after goal in their goolies. Bloody rascal!'

Dhui let out another roar. As Herbert flung himself flat before him he saw, one after another, hitherto family photos-only assuming all three dimensions and thitherto becoming people who then tossed him from hand to hand, as though playing ball. Heirless Keshab and Harinath, entirely engrossed in an endless blood-barfing contest. 'If this one wants one barrel of booze scented with jasmine juice,' grumbled Dhui, 'then that one wants two barrels with a banana bouquet. Their booze used to come from Chandernagore. *Liberty, Equality, Fraternity!*'

'Then?'

'Quiet! Once the booze competition starts, it never stops. Runs on and on till time runs out. Glug!'

'I beg you, please, please don't go away at glug.'

'Want to know more, eh? All right then—see that fellow over there, the one with the iron ring round his cock, jumping up and down? Do you know who he is?'

'Please, no, my lord.'

'Why would you? You'll only know the dirty debauched *lady doctor*. He is the great renunciate, Gopal-lal. Do you have any questions?'

'Why did he renounce?'

'Why? Why? You really want to know?'

'I do.'

'Because the cook's shelter-given daughter began a belly.'

A headless creature came wailing up to them and then proceeded to break wind and shit.

'Who's that man?'

'Not man—ask: Who's that sisterfucker? That's the adopted son, Jhulanlal. He's the one whose throat was slashed by Biharilal to give birth to Peeyu Kahaan and your father. And there, in the distance, see that man playing ludo with Queen Victoria? Go, go touch your head to his toenails once. He's Banarasilal. Ran a roaring trade with the foreigners. Supplied *native* whores to horny Englishmen.'

'Then?'

'Then? Then a long line of bokachoda-buffoons. But yes, our wives were good wives. Not too many that were fairy-like and fine, one or two at most, but mainly elephantine. Them I'll show you another day.'

Suddenly, Lambodar leapt down before him— nothing to him but a behemoth belly. Herbert reverently flung himself to the ground.

'Want to be free? Herbert! Loser! Lose your soul! Pray to Shyama or Dakshina Kalika. Kring kring kring hu hu hring hring—'

'Cut the crap,' said Sridhar, 'The only one to pray to is Adyakali, the original and only Kali, no one else. Haru, dear, dear Haradhan . . .'

Hring kring kring parameshwari swaha!

Herbert's head was reeling. Kring kring hail the secret Kali kring dring sri the funeral Kali Om Kali only Kali frightful-figured engrossed-enthralled-and-enflamed-eyed Kali impatient-for-the-taste-of-flesh-and-blood Kali. The adopted son, the throat-slit Jhulanlal, dances on, dances on, headless and heedless and his bottom still sticky with shit. Suddenly suit-clad long-late Lalitkumar appears, shouting, 'Light! Light!' while downstairs never-late Girishkumar shrieks the hour with 'Peeyu kahaan, peeyu kahaan!' and by the time this episode draws to a close Dhui the sky-skimmer is shrinking from minute to minuscule until he is no more than a deadly drop-molecule yet his voice keeps growing and yell-bellowing until it is well beyond the decibels that the human ear is able to endure: 'Herbert, you'll burn on a wood pyre ... Herbert, you'll burn on a wood fire ... Herbert, you'll burn on a wood pyre ... Herbert, you'll burn on a wood fire ...'

*

17 May 1992. A letter arrived for Herbert. A letter typed on white paper. A letter that read thus:

Dear Sir,

We have come to know of your 'supernatural' prowess from both the press and public reports—hence, this letter from us to you. We, the members of the Rationalist Association, have for quite a few years now been exposing the people-fooling fraudulent feats of many saints and sages, many astrologers, and godmen. We are not interested in how well you know our activities in this regard. As far as you are concerned, what we wish to avow is that establishing contact with dead souls is also nothing but fraud. The business you are conducting by exploiting the weakness of people is a sham. On 25 May, my colleagues and I will visit your office around 2 in the afternoon. Reporters from the two newspapers that carried reports about you will also be present. If within three days of receiving this letter, you do not contact our offices with the promise of ceasing this trickery with immediate effect and do not submit in writing a confession that your 'supernatural' activities are in truth merely a charade, then we will be forced to assume that you have accepted our challenge.

Yours truly,

Pranab Ghosh

General Secretary, West Bengal Rationalist Association

Herbert flung the letter aside.

'Illi! Fucking willy! So many big-big people, lawyers, doctors, everyone believed but now all of a sudden blam, it's a sham! Some strand of pubic hair from somewhere—

and I have to go to him and confess. Why? I am a monkey and you're my uncle? Carbuncle! Who are you? Over the nest a fuck-you flew. Oh my darling Clementine, your eyes so blue, your hair so fine! Come, come you goo-gorgers, such a tale I'll tell you your balls'll jingle bells-jingle bells. Not making any trouble, not stepping out nowhere, not needling anyone, just got a dream and set up shop—and those bastards are burning up inside! This is why the Bengalis are going to hell! Good, let them!'

Herbert returns, with great gusto, to the adventures of *Gopal Bhaar at the Spooks' Soiree.*

Eight

Like the thugee, swift and sudden,
    grab his throat and squeeze
In an instant send 'fore Death
    the one thirsting for release

                —*Pramathanath Roychowdhury*

Monday, 25 May 1992. Herbert had left word at the tea shop that he'd need a few cups of tea sent across later. A client had come that morning too. From Bardhhaman. Herbert told him, sorry, not today. Told him, come back next week. Then he'd dusted the shelves, tidied his books. Requested Nirmala to sweep the room. Marik had given his word that he'd come as soon as he was back from Madras. So, the plan was progressing. That Marik man was a generous fellow, with a heart as deep and wide as a river. Even before they'd started, how much he'd spent on whisky and cigarettes. A heartless man would never have done so much.

Herbert had never imagined that so many of them would come in the afternoon. After an early bath and lunch, he'd thought he'd take a nap. But sleep refused to come. He read their letter again. Read and read and his lips curled in a contemptuous smile. There was a fly in the room. It buzzed against the windowpane. Crawled a step or two. Then flew a circle or two. Then came back and buzzed against the windowpane again. Herbert was contemplating what happened to flies when they died when Pachu from the tea shop escorted them in.

'Here, the office. Kaka-babu, they're looking for you. When I heard it was you they wanted, I walked them over.'

So many people! Six or seven boys. Some with glasses. Beards. Shoulder bags. Two girls. Without stopping to say a word they just kept surging in. Herbert saw, outside, a tall boy in thick glasses pointing a finger at his signboard above the door, pointing it out to a girl in a salwar-kameez. The girl reached into her shoulder bag and pulled out a camera, twisted the lens like a black gun muzzle, and clicked.

One man said, 'So you're Herbert Sarkar.' Then: 'Pranab-da, please come in.'

The room had only one chair. On it sat Pranab Ghosh. So this was the man who had written the letter. The girl in the salwar-kameez walked in. And immediately, in a flurry of camera flashes, took photographs of Herbert, of his room. Herbert slid to a corner of the bed.

Moved his pillows. Asked the rest to sit beside him. One or two sat. Some others stashed themselves against the wall. The one in jeans and shirt who came in a little later, Herbert had thought that person was a man. That one now took out a cassette-tape recorder, pressed the *Record* button and placed it beside Herbert on the bed.

Pranab Ghosh took off his glasses. Without the high-powered lenses, his eyes seemed almost blank.

His voice, when he began speaking, was deep.

'Since you never came to us, it is obvious that you have accepted our *challenge*.'

The letter had contained that same word, *challenge*. But the word left Pranab Ghosh's mouth with such a sharp edge to it that Herbert felt a stab at his breast.

'No, actually, don't write-fight much. Don't even know where your office is. So I thought, what'll I do by going there anyway? Besides, what crime have I committed that I have to go at all? Not been well, either. Had dengue. Just sat up.'

'That's all very well. But what you just said, that you've committed no crime—that's an outright lie. You have committed a terrible crime. And you are still committing it.'

'What I've committed, if I really have committed it, why don't you tell me what it is. Wait, wait—let me open the window. It's too hot in here.'

'No crime? Planfully people-cheating by spouting nonsense and milking them for money—and you say you've committed no crime?'

'Who did I cheat? Let the bastard come and say, put a hand to his heart and say, I've cheated him!'

An angry Herbert had begun to shout. One of the boys said, his voice calm and cold, 'Here, don't raise your voice. Don't use *slang*.' Then turned to the camera-clicking girl and said, 'See, as soon as you *expose* them, they begin to scream and shout. They think that all this *melodrama* will help them get away with it.'

'*But he seems to be a dud*,' replied the girl. 'Although, Mickey, his profile's a lot like Monty Clift's, no?'

The girl called Mickey burst into peal-peals of laughter.

'*Oh, he's a sweet, cute, small-time crook.*'

Even Pranab Ghosh was laughing now. '*Exactly!*'

Herbert got angrier. 'Don't think your English talking scares me! Fucking English!'

Now it was Pranab Ghosh's turn to raise his voice a little. 'Shall I give you proof? Of your cheating?'

'Give, no—if you have the guts to give, give.'

'A foreign woman called Tina paid you a visit—yes?'

Beautiful young Belgian actress Tina. So beautiful. Blue-blue eyes. Pretty trills of laughter. Only, when she spoke of her mother, those eyes brimmed over with tears, her laughter lay down in sorrow—how Herbert's heart had ached for her.

'Yes, she did. A doctor came with her—I forget his name.'

'What you told Tina—I have the *cassette*. Want to hear it?'

Herbert was at a loss to understand any of this. What was happening? Why was it happening?

Pranab Ghosh takes out the *cassette* in the recorder. Puts in another. Presses *Play* and *Fast Forward* together, so there emerges a strange set of squeaks and eeks, shrieks and squawks. He quickly presses *Stop*, then *Play* again. Tina's laughter. Herbert's voice: 'Very good. Very good.' Doctor's laughter. Sounds from the street. *Stop. Fast Forward*. The cassette gyre-gimbles onward. *Stop. Play*. Herbert hears his own voice: 'Yes, such are these inexplicable arrangements. But her mother is well, I see. On the fifth plane, where the moderately virtuous dwell. O Doctor, tell her, tell her not to be sad at all. After all, how many succeed in climbing to that fifth floor? Most manage at most to scramble to the first or second only. But her mother's run really far, I tell you, Doctor. One more floor and such eternal joy—just one more floor and she'll be free!'

Doctor: 'Let me tell her what you've just said.'

Herbert: 'Yes, yes, tell her. Let her be happy.'

Doctor: '*He is saying that your mother is now on the fifth plane which is the realm of beings with moderate virtues.*'

Tina: '*What, oh yes, how exciting, tell him that he is marvellous, a master . . .*'

Doctor: 'Tina is saying that you possess extraordinary powers.'

Stop.

Pranab Ghosh takes out the *cassette*. Puts back the first one. Rubs his glasses with his handkerchief and puts them on. Presses *Record* again. 'Do you know who Tina really is? A member of the Geneva-based international rationalist movement. That Tibetan lama in London, the one with all the politicians in his pocket—trapped by Tina and now languishing in jail. In Mexico, Brazil, the Philippines—do you know how many miracle-men she has proven to be frauds? We're the ones who sent her to you. To let her see one of our typical specimens.'

'How can that be? There was that doctor with her, explaining what I was saying.'

'That doctor? Yes, Alok is most certainly a doctor. And a founding member of our organization.'

'So what, for god's sake.'

'So what? So we have proved that you are a cheat. A bujrook-bigcrook. Tina's mother is hale and hearty—and alive! And you packed her up and moved her off right onto the fifth plane? *Apart from that*, you're obviously illiterate—you don't have a spot of the *sophistication* required to efficiently pull of this kind of thing. If you did, you wouldn't have spelt Shanta as Santa. Bimalendu is part of a famous *theatre group*. He came to you too— yes, yes, that trunk with the sister's body *in so many pieces*. He *clearly marked* how uncomfortable you were *at the mention of* Lalbazar. So. Now, it's your call. What will you call yourself, Mr Conversations with the Dead?'

'More like Major General of the Crap Corps!' says one of the bearded boys.

And everyone roars with laughter. Herbert breaks out in a sweat. Grows red in the face. Pulls out from the shelf *Accounts of the Afterlife* and *Mysteries of the Afterlife*.

'Ever heard of these, have you? You really think it's all fraud? Read, read and then see if you understand, what the different plans are, what the different arrangements are.'

'We don't need to read any of that.'

'Same old *planchette*,' said the camera girl, flipping through *Accounts of the Afterlife*, 'same old *spirits*. *Bullshit*.'

'Won't look,' shouted Herbert, 'won't learn! Only gad about all afternoon, barge into people's houses and fight—aren't you ashamed?'

'You'll know who's the one to be ashamed when the police come and drag you away.'

'Why, why will the police drag me? So easy it is?'

'Yes, it is indeed so easy. Because that ugh-doom bug-doom bullshit that you fed Tina, you fed it to a lot of others and got a lot of money. That is *cheating*. That is theft. Wait and see what happens when we hand in our *report*.'

'What'll happen?'

'The police will come. And *arrest* you.'

'No! The police won't come! I had a dream. Binu was killed by the police. Binu was shot by the police.'

Herbert began to scream at the top of his lungs, began to weep and wail: 'The police won't come. I didn't lie. Ghosts have been. They always will be.'

At a sign from Pranab Ghosh, the girl clicked photo after photo of Herbert having hysterics. Then lit a cigarette. Outside the door, a crowd of the neighbourhood boys. Even they daren't come forward. All the police-police had made them wary.

'The best medicine for such samples is Stalin,' said one of the boys stashed against the wall, 'If only he'd fallen into Stalin's hands. *Straight firing squad*.'

'All that Lenin–Stalin even I know, OK?' shouted a Herbert now in the cold grip of terror, 'The police won't come. The police don't hurt the innocent. The police will catch you instead. I can see the God of Death circling you already.'

'All right. We're off. But as soon as we get Tina's *report*, we'll make our *move*.'

'Shut up! Fucking English! I'll also do what I have to do! Only fucking English! Ever seen a double chang? Eh? Seen a double chang?'

'Do whatever you want. But know this, we will not spare you nor any other swindler like you. Wipe out every tantrick and godman we can find. Not spare even one.'

'All right, all right, we'll see who does what.'

It is not clear whom Herbert meant when he said *we*. As they began to walk out of the room, he began to whirl about in a frenzy: 'Oh, oh, how I fucked them well and good! *Cat, bat, water, dog, fish! Cat, bat, water, dog, fish!*'

The whirling makes him dizzy. He bumps against the bed. Falls to the floor. Gets up. The more afraid he grows, the more he rampage-rages. He begins to drip with sweat. Suddenly he stops, stares at Binu's bed, mattress, pillows. Binu had been shot by the police. Would the police kill him too? And Tina! Who could imagine a woman so wretched? Such a sinful girl! So, this, this is what lay in your heart?

'Cat, bat, water, dog, fish, cat, bat, water, dog, fish, cat, bat, water, dog, fish, cat, bat . . .'

Outside, on the street, they were walking away, Pranab Ghosh more or less in the centre of their group. 'Pranab-da,' said Mickey, 'I must say that the man was very *crude*.'

'So? You can be as crude as you want in this country, but you'll never run short of clients.'

'Remember that levitation case in Baruipur?' one of the boys said, 'What was that chap's name?'

'Moslayuddin?'

'Yes, yes, Moslayuddin. Now that man was *tremendous* smart.'

'Well, then, if you must, I think the *really clever pack* was that lot.'

'Which lot, Pranab-da? Those Tarapith ones?'

'No, no, those other ones, seven astrologers, on TV—remember?'

'Oh yes, but Pranab-da, they were *totally urban*. No wonder they were smart.'

'But isn't Herbert *urban* too?'

They have no answer. They say nothing. Pranab Ghosh says nothing too. Then: 'Sometimes I *wonder* why people do these things. You will be mistaken if you think that, like Casanova, all of these men have a carefully laid-out plan.'

Mickey was surprised. 'Which Casanova, Pranab-da?'

'The Casanova you know, *the great lady killer*. He was clever indeed. Passed himself off as an *occultist* in order to impress the girls. But what about Cagliostro—what was his motive? Rasputin, on the other hand, is easy to explain. He'd managed to impress even Goethe. *Great rascal*. There's also the Count of St Germain. *Fascinating*. In *comparison*, what can we call the fellow we've seen? Gopal Fool.'

He who'd written the letter, the photographer and the reporter, the college boys and girls—after they had all gone, Koton, Borka, Koka, Gyanobaan, Buddhiman, Somnath, Abhay, Khororobi's brother Jhaapi, Gobindo— all the boys rushed into the room and saw Harbert shivering. Gasping-clasping-unclasping, sweating. His shirt he'd thrown off. The table-fan swung from side to side, and with it swung Herbert, trying to catch the breeze. They stopped it swinging, made him sit on his bed, made him drink a glass of water. Sent for tea, special tea, until slowly, Herbert began to calm down. But the fear wouldn't leave his eyes. He kept saying, 'It's all become a googly, all a googly! Oof, thumping inside, thump-thumping inside . . . My god, what bandobast is this?'

Nine

Impenetrable, impassable void, unseeing eyes
Such flames! Such fumes! Beyond—what lies?

—*Akshay Kumar Boral*

9 a.m. 9.30. 10. The signboard-stripped door refused to open, so they began to knock and bang. Koka, Borka, Somnath came running, their eyes still heavy with sleep, their mouths still stinking of the night before.

'Herbert-da! Herbert-da!'

The knocking and the shouting was loud enough to be heard on the first floor. Dhanna told Phuchka, 'Go once and see, no.'

Phuchka went, one cheek still covered with shaving cream. He was a businessman, a practical man. He quickly figured that something was wrong. He was the one who told them to break the door. The door was broken in—and the smell of death that had festered all night burst out into the open with a whoosh. Phuchka ran back upstairs. Told Dhanna. Dhanna, dazed and disoriented, began to scream: 'Killed himself! My brother's killed himself!'

Dhanna-boudi and Nirmala rushed downstairs. Then, crying, slowly climbed back up. Jyathaima had not understood, at first. Then she'd fainted in shock. It is impossible to tell which happy memory had flashed across Girishkumar's mind when he spotted the crowds outside the house. But a 'Peeyu kahaan! Peeyu kahaan!' reminded everyone of his presence.

Gobi, Hartal, etc.—Dhanna's friends arrived.

'Hey, don't touch the body. Don't touch nothing in the room.'

'Open the window, Hartal-da?'

'Didn't I tell you to touch nothing? *Suicide* case. Any-one touches anything and the cops'll tie their testicles in a knot.'

Dhanna came down again, crying. A band of boys and bicycles sped off to the police station. The officer heard them out. Then, 'Bloody bastard!' he said, 'Ruined my day.'

Herbert was unfazed. Unmoved. Now forever unconcerned with the trifling troubles of this world.

The crowds continued to swell.

Koka, Somnath, Gobindo—how-howled in grief.

'Just last night he paid for a TV. Spent so much. If only we'd known, even a little . . .'

Khororobi's brother Jhaapi was looking as though he were *mentally unstable*. Ever since his brother's case, he'd been a little funny-funny. Now he squatted on the pavement and shouted every now and then, 'Over! All over!'

In only a little while the police van arrived. An officer and three constables. The crowd parted to let them through.

The officer inspected the room and the body. 'Any suicide note-fote?'

No one could tell.

Pinching his nose tight, the officer went over to Herbert lying flat and still, reached into his breast pocket and pulled out a fold of paper.

On it was written:

The tank-trapped tilapiya is off to the sea
Want to see a double chang? A double chang?
Cat, bat, water, dog, fish.

'Never read a suicide note like this in my whole bloody life,' said the officer, 'Was he mad or what?'

'Not mad , really,' said Hartal, 'A little touched, perhaps.'

Local Dr Sudhir refused to sign the *death certificate*. 'He was my patient, it's true,' he said, 'But he didn't die of *dengue*. Nor did he die of my *treatment*. He died by committing *suicide, and that too in a ghastly manner.* The police've come. Now, kindly, please do not *request* me any more. We're neighbours, don't forget. If I could write off two lines and help you out, do you think I wouldn't have?'

Thereafter the boys would always think of him as Dr Sonofabitch.

Finally, the police officer said, 'All right. I'm going back to the station, sending a corpse car. One of you come with me. The constables will stay back, keep watch.'

'You won't come back, sir?'

'Of course I will! Let me speak to Sambhunath Hospital, if I can get him on their list, then from there straight to Katapukur morgue.'

'Sir, when will we get the *body*?'

'Let's see, what time is it now? Quarter to twelve . . . Say, seven? Why don't you come to the morgue by seven? Although with morgues you can never tell . . . it may end up taking longer.'

'Oh, you don't worry about that. We'll figure out how to hurry things up there.'

'Then there's nothing to worry about, then.'

A black corpse-car carried Herbert away. On the first-floor veranda, Nirmala and Dhanna-boudi watched him drive away, Jyathaima clutched between them. The sun was high in the sky. So strong and fierce that the calls of the crows dried up in their throats.

Up on the roof, beneath the scorching sun, Lalit-kumar told his wife, 'Shobha! Will the film be a hit or a miss? It will be exactly as you say. I am happy to accept your choice.'

Shobharani laughs and laughs, shakes and shimmies with laughter.

Downstairs, the sweeper arrived, took out the bucket and threw the bloody water down the drain. Threw away the bottles, the cutlet bones, the dead cockroaches, the blade, the cigarette butts, the ash. Gulped down the last few drops of rum.

The room was washed. The windows flung open. The fly trapped in the room since the night before perched for a moment on the window grille. Then buzzed a few circles in the air. Then flew away.

The neighbourhood boys held a meeting and decided that Herbert's bed and mattress would be used to take him on his final journey. Ever since the Saha-da– Swapan case, the crematorium was insisting on burning the dead's bed and bedding too. Let Herbert-da's bed go with him.

But Dhanna-dada's permission was vital in this regard.

'I was thinking the same thing,' Dhanna said gravely, 'It's so full of him, best it goes with him.'

Then he began to reminisce. 'That bed, that mattress, all bought for Binu. Binu died an unnatural death. And now Haru is gone too. What now? Take it, take it all. But, yes, the bed is a hurdy-sturdy one. You want to take that also?'

'So many more beds will come, Dhanna-dada. Let this one go. All his time he spent on it.'

'Take it,' sighed Dhanna, 'We'll go to the crematorium too. Oh, and you boys had better take some money. There will be expenses, after all.'

'Don't worry about all that, Dhanna-dada. Herbert-da was our brother too. We'll arrange for the car and all. Please, we beg you, don't make a fuss now.'

Dhanna begins to cry again.

The boys get busy organizing things.

Lala in the neighbourhood had a fleet of lorries. So a lorry and a driver were easy. Then came the flowers, incense-sticks, *scent*, clothes—everything. The bed was lifted onto the lorry. Then the mattress. The mattress was really heavy. They struggled quite a bit.

'Old-fashioned stuff, see? Packed full with coir. Feel the *weight*?'

Sticks of tuberoses were tied to the four legs of the bed. The mattress covered with a new sheet. A new pillow placed upon it. In the end so many boys had gathered that they had to hire a small Tempo. The rest of the neighbourhood who wanted to go had been told to go directly to the crematorium.

This lot set off for the morgue.

A huge crowd gathered to bid farewell to the lorry-and-Tempo sorrow convoy. Onward, captain: Destination—Remount Road, Katapukur. In-between, sips of country liquor. A blast down the throat, raw, then the bottle tucked away at the waist. The towel tied tightly over it again.

However, in the matter of alleviating their own sorrows, the spirits may be found to be entirely subservient or helpless. Therefore, some spirits, unable to endure that unbearable agony, manifest themselves before their near and dear ones, or, remaining invisible, send them manifold portents, in an attempt to urge them to perform those funereal rites which will ensure that they, the spirits, are able to rest in peace. This particular power of the spirits is remarkably well known to those who are experts in this regard. The English experts, and the Bengali experts—both have spoken of this power, both have deliberated upon it, and both have not been averse to writing a variety of books to communicate their thoughts about it.

—*Mysteries of the Afterlife*

At the morgue, after the autopsy, the loss-of-blood examination and the stitching back up, when Herbert emerged all wrapped in a sheet, he looked quite neat and tidy—not grisly and grotesque like most suicides. Just before this, across the western sky, the slowly sliding sun's bewitching bloody glow had touched every cloud with tenderness. The pond just beside the morgue, behind that the long lines of the railway tracks, and along them, along that field, the *wagon-breakers* flashing past like deer.

Gobindo, one of the boys, came from a rich home. Emptying a bottle of expensive scent all over Herbert's body, he shouted, 'Let the other dumb deads smell of shit. For our boss, only *Intimate* will do!'

The lorry rolls on. And suddenly, the *slogans* begin:

'Long live Herbert-da!'

'Long live—long, long live!'

'Won't forget you, Herbert-da! Won't forget!'

'Won't forget, never forget!'

The lorry paused in traffic. 'Which *party* was he a *leader* of?' someone asked.

'*Band party*,' someone answered.

Then the clapping started. Along with the whistling and weird cries and shouts. Thus, through the final ritual, was grief gradually transformed into a happy hullaballoo. No one noticed. They were not meant to. By the time the lorry drew up to the gates of the crematorium, the lights had been switched on. It was night. Beside the gates were waiting a weeping Shobharani and a dumbfounded Lalitkumar. But as he heard the sounds of the mourners' exhilaration, Lalitkumar could not help himself: 'Why are you crying, Shobha? But, look, look at this *carnival!*'

Dhanna, Phuchka and Bulan, the neighbourhood *seniors*, they had reached already. They were waiting too. Someone ran off to do the paperwork. Those who accompany the dead to the crematorium, they often like to make enquiries about how and why the other corpses died. One such man asked Koka, and a mildly intoxicated Koka replied thus:

'What happened, brother?'

'What happened to whom?'

'I mean, what happened to your brother?'

'*Murder.*'

Koka thought that the word for death in English was *murder*. In Bengali, people die. In English, they *murder*.

Once this word was out, a huge crowd swarmed down upon them for a glimpse of the *murder-case*. Even those maintaining ritual contact with their dead, even they began to fiddle and fidget, waiting for their turn to scramble over and see.

Dhanna, a drained and desolate Dhanna, said he couldn't do it. Couldn't bring himself to perform the last rites. So nephew Bulan was the one who touched the fire to Herbert's mouth. The crematorium was crammed with policemen. Bits of talk, shouted slogans, sobbing.

'Yes, yes, the mattress and pillow go with him.'

'Herbert-da, long live Herbert-da!'

'Boss, you're going away!'

'As long as sun and moon shall shine, Herbert— your name shall shine!'

'Please move, please move, the corpse is going in!'

Clatter clatter clatter—the door to the furnace rolled open—clatter. Herbert, sleeping his final sleep, waits for a few seconds. The slogans rise to a crescendo. Crash through the crematorium. As the bed of flames deep in the heart of the furnace blazed into view, an entranced Lalitkumar whispered, '*Fascinating!*'

'Quiet, bastard!' someone roared back, and a simultaneously startled and shaken Lalitkumar turned his head and saw Dhui beside him and a little further away,

Lambodar, Sridhar, Nishapati, Keshab, headless Jhulan-lal—all of them standing, waiting.

Herbert rattled and rolled into the furnace. His clothes, his hair and the sheet that covered him burst into flame. Clatter clatter clatter—the door to the furnace rolled shut—clatter. And then only an unbroken hum as the fire burnt within.

A little to the back of the crowd stood a forlorn Surapati Marik. Two English-newspaper *cuttings* folded in his pocket. 'Farewell, friend, farewell,' he thought to himself and lit a cigarette.

People, so many people, a wave, swelling down to the ground.

The furnace hums on.

Suddenly, a small explosion. Like a bucket-covered chocolate bomb bursting. Boom!

Before the trace of it has completely disappeared, there is another. Louder. Boom! Then another, yet another. One after the other. Louder, and louder. The doors of the furnace begin to shiver and shake, the crowds begin to panic and pell-mell. The on-duty policemen scramble to their feet.

And—TI-DOOM!

Part of the ceiling above the furnace explodes, launching bricks and sand and chunks of plaster everywhere, and through that hole billow multicoloured plumes of smoke, reeking of gunpowder and explosives.

'Bloody *charge!*' a local goon roars, 'Bloody *charge!*'

'Switch it off!' one of the policemen, displaying an astonishing presence of mind, finally manages to shout, 'They're bursting inside!'

But at that very moment a sky-splitting explosion rips out the walls beside and behind the furnace. Bits of hot coil fall into pots of funeral water and hiss and sizzle and smoke. The lights go out. The destroyed furnace smoulders red.

An awful affair.

People rush about in the dark. Someone in one of the houses opposite must have telephoned. The police arrive. More police arrive. Cordon off the entire crematorium. Much later, when the CESC people manage to patch together an emergency electrical connection and the lights came back on, the furnace was found to have been exploded from within, blown entirely to bits.

In the end, deep at night, under the eagle eye of the police, Herbert's head, entrails, arms and legs, belly and breast—all the bits and pieces are collected and taken to the next-door *manual* set-up and burnt on a wood fire; a wood pyre.

*

That Herbert's body was jigsawed together and burnt led to a lot of debate and discussion during the initial phases of the investigation. Only but natural. After the events of 21 May 1991, everyone had reason enough to believe that, comparable to Dhanu, the LTTE's *live human bomb*, Herbert had been *a dead human bomb*. Although his motive was not entirely clear. In fact, at first glance, there seemed to be no motive at all. Because that night no prominent personality had been expected at the crematorium. And even if they had been . . . the veteran investigators simply dismissed that hypothesis.

Actually, when one particular event ends up having a profound impact, all subsequent events are attempted to be explained in its light. Such is human nature.

> The tank-trapped tilapiya is off to the sea
> Want to see a double chang? A double chang?
> *Cat, bat, water, dog, fish.*
>
> —Herbert Sarkar

Even the suicide note didn't seem to contain any coded messages, although in the challenge of the double chang a threatening tone was more than evident. Let the record show that in some areas of Howrah, especially venal swines and sons-of-bitches were indeed referred to as double changs. But 'Cat, bat, water, dog, fish!' Possibly nothing more than mere whimsy. The man had been *exposed* by then. A *severe shock*, followed by the inevitable *depression*. And, of course, he'd been *abnormal* all along.

Still, it is not possible for a mystery so rife with the reek of gunpowder to remain inexplicable and irresolute. Such a state of affairs is not desirable for either state or time or people. In fact, such a state is particularly undesirable.

*

The crematorium catastrophe was all Binu's fault. Yes, Binu the dead Naxalite. Night after night, it had been Binu and his friends who'd packed every inch of the mattress with dynamite sticks stolen from the ICI factory at Gomiah, dynamite sticks of varying lengths and force, meant for blowing apart rocks and mountains. These advanced sticks were built to withstand considerable *shock* without exploding. Not crude handmade bombs these, that a little pressure and presto! they popped. Who is not aware of the positive role played by dynamite in ensuring the progress of this great nation?

Perhaps Binu and his friends had planned an awful apocalyptic affair. Perhaps, perhaps the assassination of some prominent personality. Perhaps some even more unimaginable calamity. That had remained undone. That had remained undone, true, but for the last 20-odd years, that assortment of explosives had lain winter-sleeping tight inside the mattress and then, warmed awake by the flames of the furnace, exploded into angry life.

And what is even more astonishing is that if, since 18 May 1992, the practice of burning the bed along with the dead had not been established, then none of this would have happened.

How strange, then, was this detonation!

The deplorable turn of events that unfolded around the cremation of Herbert's bloodless body inescapably signal that when and how an explosion will occur, and who will cause that explosion—of all such knowledge the state machinery remains woefully ignorant still.

Ten

In vain we come, in vain we go
To what end? We do not know.

—Akshay Kumar Boral

Without the bed, Herbert's room looked very empty and large. Although no one had observed it thus, for it was put under lock and key and stayed that way for a long time thereafter. Then, much later, one night, in a pitch-black *loadshedding*-dark night, there had been a terrible storm. The window that had been opened, the window through which the fly had flown, that window had remained open. The storm wind, the wild wind bellowed through the room and scattered all over it the pages, beginning from 171, of *Accounts of the Afterlife*. A bolt of lightning scorched with its reflection Herbert's mirror on the wall shelf. Raging, the wind swung the hanging Ulster up and down. *Mysteries of the Afterlife*, *Gopal Bhaar at the Spooks' Soiree*, Herbert's notebook of poems, Shanta's letter, the West Bengal Rationalist Association's letter—the wind blew right through them, set them all aflutter. Flung the shirt and dhuti and towel from the line on which they'd hung and flew them to the floor.

A few days later, Dhanna-dada unlocked the room and sold all the books, the pages of the books, the notebook, the signboard made of tin—sold them all to a scrap merchant. Sent the table fan and trunk and chair up to the first floor. The trunk contained a broken *dot pen* and a few coins. Herbert's umbrella and Ulster were given away to the bathroom cleaner and a beggar, respectively. In the heat of a summer afternoon, the beggar had been reluctant to accept that blanket-like cloak-like object but then, thinking of the future, he finally relented. That same beggar was also gifted Herbert's shirt and dhuti and towel. The scrap merchant who'd bought the signboard had at first found himself in a bit of a fix. But then, by the grace of good fortune, it was bought by a pop-gun-and-balloon man in New Market who devised an elaborate hammering of nails all over it to which he then tied many multicoloured balloons. Thus Herbert's signboard became a target for pop-gun pellets.

Once all the balloons had burst, then through the jungle of nails, perhaps the eye could see the upside-down letters: Conversations with the Dead. Prop: Herbert Sarkar.

Perhaps many days later, perhaps many, many years later, some little boy, letting go of his mother's hand, his father's hand, will run and run and then stand still before the dusty glass window of some antique shop and stare and stare, entranced, at the light-holding fairy still standing on the other side. And when his mother, his father, when they drag him away, perhaps his lower lip will tremble a little with hurt.

None of this, of course, may ever happen.

But if it does, then later, even later, when the boy begins to shiver in his sleep, even then no one will notice. That sort of thing happens all the time.

Even, even later, perhaps a cut-loose kite will flit and float across this sky and that, and then drift down to rest on Herbert's top-terrace. No one will ever know how the morning mist makes the top-terrace seem so very unclear, so very unreasonable.

Or, if that little boy ever runs a fever, if that fever makes him delirious, as fevers are wont to do, then if anyone listens to his words, perhaps they may come to hear of a certain fairy.

It is also possible that they may not.

The windows are closed in Herbert's empty room. If the wild wind comes again, there is nothing left for it to toss and tumble. Such is life.

Red balloons, blue balloons—they all fall down. New balloons are blown up and tied with string again. They all fall down again. Such is life meant to be.

Perhaps the little boy will whimper and weep as he sleeps. Then giggle and laugh. When children do this, the grown-ups say they are dream-delighting with the gods.

He talks in his sleep every night. Perhaps the doctor will prescribe some pills. Perhaps the doctor will reassure the parents, 'Let him sleep. He'll be all right if he sleeps.'

That sleep never all-rights anything was known only too well by Lalitkumar and Shobharani. Because even after their uninterrupted and blissful sleep, even after Herbert was born, even after a vast array of joys and sorrows, in the end, the film had been a *flop*.

A *flop* film has no *picture*. Only *sound*. Growing faint and more faint and so faint that you can barely hear the words:

> *Cat, bat, water, dog, fish . . .*
> *Cat, bat, water, dog, fish . . .*
> *Cat, bat, water, dog, fish . . .*
> *Cat, bat, water, dog, fish . . .*

TRANSLATOR'S NOTES

PAGE 2, *Corporation tap*: The Kolkata Municipal Corporation or KMC (formerly Calcutta Municipal Corporation or CMC), established in 1876, is responsible for the civic infrastructure and administration of the city of Kolkata, including water purification and supply. The water spouts set up by them in every neighbourhood are referred to as Corporation taps.

PAGE 2, *Herbert-da*: Dada is the Bengali word for older brother. Shortened to 'da', it is added to names to indicate that relationship both in and outside the family.

PAGE 3, *googly*: According to the BBC: 'The leg-spinner's prize weapon, bowled properly, a googly is almost undetectable [. . . it] looks like a normal leg-spinner but turns towards the batsmen, like an off-break, rather than away from the bat.' [http://news.bbc.co.uk/ sport2/hi/cricket/skills/-4173812.stm] In Bengal, a land of ardent cricket fans, the term is often used to refer an unexpected turn of events.

PAGE 7, *Gyanobaan, Buddhimaan*: The first name means The Knowledgeable One; the second, The Intelligent One.

PAGE **8**, *underwear*: In Indian English, and in many of the regional languages, this English word is used to refer specifically to a man's briefs/boxer shorts.

PAGE **8**, *scale-scraping blade*: An enormous curved blade fixed to a wooden base. Used for scraping the scales off the fish, and then for slicing it into pieces.

PAGE **8**, *peeyu kahaan*: A Hindi version of the call of the common hawk-cuckoo, or brainfever bird, meaning 'Where's my love?'

PAGE **9**, *pin you*: Bengali slang, roughly meaning 'I'll screw you.'

PAGE **10**, *full shirt*: Used in Bengali to refer to a full-sleeved shirt. Half shirt refers to a half-sleeved shirt. Full pant refers to full-length trousers while half pant refers to shorts.

PAGE **11**, *club*: Informal associations formed in each neighbourhood, which organize pujas, musical soirees, sports meets, blood-donation camps, relief work, etc. Some have a room with a TV and basic sports equipment and function as a local hangout for many of the neighbourhood boys and men.

PAGE **11**, *Bangla*: Bengali name for locally brewed alcohol.

PAGE **13**, *Isabgol*: Brand-name for a psyllium-husk preparation, one of the most commonly used laxatives in West Bengal.

PAGE **13**, *Goju Bose's expression when he finally succeeded in signing up Krishanu and Bikash for Mohun Bagan*: A reference to the legendary rivalry between two football teams from Calcutta: East Bengal Club and Mohun Bagan AC.

Between 1983 and 1991, midfielders Krishanu Dey and Bikash Panji were the star players of East Bengal, helping it win five times the prestigious Calcutta Football League—one of the oldest football tournaments in the world. The Krishanu–Biskash pair was constantly being wooed by rival Mohun Bagan and, finally, in 1992, both players, after being promised hefty fees, signed on to play for them. This was seen as a major coup inside the Calcutta football empire and even lead to several incidents of hooliganism and rioting. However, the dramatic transfer of the leading pair proved a success for Mohun Bagan, helping them win the Calcutta Football League in 1992, and put a famously jubilant smile on the face of, among others, Sajal Bose, better known by his nickname Goju, the secretary of the club.

PAGE **16,** *Ma go*: This is a bit of a bilingual pun. In English, of course, it sounds like a child babbling to go closer to its mother. But in Bengali, to add 'go' to a person's name is to underline the affection one feels for them, is to emphasize even more the intimacy of the bond. So, at once, both 'go to Ma' and 'Ma dearest'.

PAGE **18,** *English-medium*: Private school, teaching all its lessons in English. Different from and more expensive than the state-government schools teaching in Bengali.

PAGE **19,** *Bharat Sevashram Sangha*: A Hindu charitable NGO in India. Founded in 1917, it provides shelter, food, medical treatment and public-safety services to pilgrims at various places of worship and religious fairs.

PAGE **20,** *saloon*: In West Bengal, a barbershop.

PAGE 20, *nuliya*: Fisherman, also expert swimmers and divers who function as swimming guides and lifeguards for the tourists in Odisha, especially on the beaches of Puri which is both a pilgrimage site for Hindus and a very popular holiday spot.

PAGE 21, *Amrik Singh Arora*: Singer of modern, folk and devotional Bengali songs who began his career in the late 1960s singing Bollywood hits at Calcuttta's famous Blue Fox restaurant and nightclub.

PAGE 23, *Dol*: Spring festival commemorating Krishna and Radha on their swing of love, marking the day when Krishna smeared Radha's face with colour. The word dol means 'swing'.

PAGE 25, *Old Ganga*: The Adi Ganga, also known as Gobindapur Creek, Surman's Nullah and Tolly's Nullah, was the main flow of the Hooghly River from the fifteenth to the seventeenth century but has since then virtually dried up. Located immediately behind the Keoratala Crematorium in South Calcutta, it is frequently used by mourners to immerse the ashes of their dead.

PAGE 26, *Ashtami*: The Eighth Day of the Durga Puja celebrations in West Bengal. The ninth is Nabami and the tenth, Dashami, the names arising from the Bengali words for 'eighth', 'ninth', etc.

PAGE 26, *Jaya*: Another name for the goddess Durga. Hence the use of the word 'devi' ('goddess') in the letter which Khororobi writes to her.

PAGE 29, *Rabba! Rabba!* An exclamation in Punjabi, equiavalent to 'Lord! Lord!'

PAGE **31,** *Vishwakarma Puja*: A day of celebration for Vishwakarma, a Hindu god, considered to be the divine architect. In many parts of Eastern India, especially West Bengal, the holiday is an occasion to fly kites.

PAGE **31,** *manja*: Special thread for 'fighter' kites, prepared by gumming, colouring and coating with powdered glass.

PAGE **34,** *Morning Will Come Again*: *Phir Subah Hogi* (1958), Indian film produced and directed by Ramesh Saigal, starring Raj Kapoor and Mala Sinha; an adaption of Fyodor Dostoevsky's *Crime and Punishment*.

PAGE **37,** *boudi*: 'Bou' in Bengali means both bride and wife. 'Di' is a shortened form of 'didi' or older sister. Together, it is a term of endearment, and respectful address, for the woman married to one's older brother, and for a married woman by any younger person, in and outside the family.

PAGE **37,** *with money saved up from his tuitions*: Older, college-going students, often provide tuition to younger schoolgoing boys and girls as a way of earning some pocket money.

PAGES **45–6,** 'Countless revolutionary martyrs have laid down their lives . . .': From Mao Zedong, *On Coalition Government* [a political report made to the Seventh National Congress of the Communist Party of China, 24 April 1945], Section V: 'Let the Whole Party Unite and Fight to Accomplish its Tasks!' (Available online at: www.marxists.org/reference/archive/mao/selected-works/volume-3/mswv3_25.htm)]

PAGE **46,** *19 November 1970 was the night of the bloody Barasat killings*: '[E]leven Naxalites were shot dead and their bullet-ridden bodies thrown along a highway in the Barasat area . . . Bullets of service revolvers found in the bodies of the youths in the Barasat area, and other reports published [. . .] as to how they were rounded up in the Maidan area while holding a secret meeting, left hardly anybody in doubt as to the "mystery" of the massacre. . . .'— T. Goswami, cited in Dilip Hiro, *Inside India Today* (London: Routledge, 1976), p. 203.

'Following the 1971 elections, particularly in the second half of the year, the Calcutta Police, in collaboration with the Central Reserve Police, increased its offensive against the Naxalites. Regular combing of suspected areas, predawn raids on houses, extermination of sympathisers/supporters of the Communist Party of India (Marxist–Leninist) by the police became a part of the city life. According to police sources, between March 1970 and August 1971, 1,783 CPI(M–L) supporters/members were killed in Calcutta and its suburbs. Later investigators claimed the figure was at least double. Between May and December 1971, the police opened fire on Naxalite prisoners in at least six jails in West Bengal. The newly elected Congress government of West Bengal also fuelled the counter-revolutionary activities to a great extent. In response, Charu Mazumdar called upon his followers to avenge every murder of his comrades. In an amazing show of fearlessness, they struggled to put their leader's theory into practice.'—Ashoke Kumar Mukhopadhyay, 'Through the Eyes of the Police', *Economic and Political Weekly* 41(29) (22 July 2006).

PAGE **46**, *Charu Majumder.* Father of the Naxalite movement. Wrote, during 1965–66, various articles based on Marx-Lenin-Mao thought, the 'Historic Eight Documents' which went on to form the basis of the Naxalite movement. Founded the CPI(M–L) in 1969 after the Naxalbari Uprising (25 May)— a peasants' uprising at Naxalbari in Darjeeling, during which they began to forcefully recapture their lands. He died in police custody in 1972.

PAGE **46**, *in his communiqué dated 22 November 1970*: Charu Majumder, 'Avenge The Heroic Martyrs' (27 October 1970):

[. . .] The incident at Barasat clearly shows how isolated from the people are these assassins and how panic-stricken and scared out of their wits are they. They had not the courage to face these youths even after getting their hands tied. That is why the assassins fired five or six shots at every one of these youths and killed them one by one. This gang of cowards knows that those whom they are murdering today are immortal sons of India—worthy of begin respected by every country, every nation. That is why the cowards murdered these youths, who knew no fear of death, in the darkness of the night and left their dead bodies on the roadside.

None of those political parties which are today carrying on a dog-fight among themselves for ministerial offices, shedding crocodile tears for the martyrs, and trying to utilize these murders in the fight for votes, can escape responsibility for the murders. The hands of each of them are dyed in the blood of the martyrs. They all are providing political arguments in justification of the murder of the revolutionaries and are secretly supplying the police with information about the whereabouts of the revolutionaries.

[. . .]

Every revolutionary cadre should take the resolve to avenge the heroic martyrs. These butchers are enemies of the Indian people, enemies of progress and lackeys of foreigners. The Indian people will not be liberated until these butchers are liquidated.

The author may have mistaken the date of publication. Available at cpiml.org/library/charu-mazumdar-collected-writings/historic-magurjan-birth-of-great-peoples-liberation-army-27-october-1970/avenge-the-heroic-martyrs/.

PAGE 49, *The Patriot* and *The Southern Country*: *The Patriot* is a translation of *Deshabrati*, the principal Naxalite journal. *The Southern Country* is a translation of *Dakshin Desh*, both the name of a magazine and the group that published it, a group which advocated/promoted armed agrarian revolution based on Mao's thought, in place of parliamentary democracy.

PAGE 52, *Police dog, Debi Roy*: Chief of the Detective Department of Calcutta Police at the time, and notorious for his leading role in the violent repression of the Naxal movement in Calcutta.

PAGE 53, *roll shop*: The roll—eggs, onions and/or a skewer (or kathi, from the Bengali word for 'stick') of grilled chicken rolled up in a paratha—is a common roadside snack in

Calcutta. The most common options at such shops would be egg roll, chicken roll, egg-chicken roll, etc.

PAGE 53, *Bhuidola*: 'Earthquake!' in a Hindi dialect.

PAGE 60, *Tarapith*: 'A *shakta pith* [seat of shakti], and the abode of the Devi's Third Eye. It is also the home of the great goddess Tara. [. . .] notorious for the unsavoury Tantric rituals and animal sacrifices which were performed in the temple. Stranger things still were rumoured to take place after sunset in the riverside burning ground on the edge of town, outside the boundaries of both village life and the conventions of Bengali society.'—William Dalrymple, *Nine Lives: In Search of the Sacred in Modern India* (London: Bloomsbury, 2009), pp. 205–6.

PAGE 60, *Ghutiari Sharif*: A tiny suburb in the hinterland of South 24-Parganas, Ghutiari Sharif boasts a *mazaar* or *dargah* of Pir Ghazi Mubarak Ali Sahab, rumoured to have kept wild tigers as pets. According to legend, sometime in the seventeenth century, this village, then part of the Sunderbans, was hit by a severe drought for several months and it was only due to Ghazi Sahab's meditation that the rains finally arrived. The residents were saved but the great man paid with his life.

PAGE 64, *Fox sisters of America*: '. . . Hydesville, New York, 1848. At the home of blacksmith John Fox, strange rapping noises began to occur in the bedroom of young daughters Margaret ("Maggie") and Katharine ("Katie"). The girls claimed the noises were communications from the departed spirit of a murdered peddler. After a time, on the night of March 31, the girls' mother witnessed a remarkable demonstration: Loudly, Katie addressed "Mr. Splitfoot," saying "do as I do," and clapping her hands. At once, there came the same number of mysterious raps. Next Maggie exclaimed, "Now do just as I do; count one, two, three, four," clapping her hands accordingly. Four raps came in response. [. . .] Before long, people discovered that the girls could conjure up not only the ghostly peddler but other obliging spirits as well. The demonstrations received such attention that the girl's older sister, Leah Fish, originated a "spiritualistic" society. Following a successful visit to New York, Leah took the girls on tour to towns and cities across the nation. Then, four decades after, sisters Margaret and Katherine confessed it had all been a trick. Margaret went on to state: "I think that it is about time that the truth of this miserable subject 'Spiritualism' should be brought out. It is now widespread all over the world, and unless it is put down it will do great evil. I was the first in the field and I have the right to expose it. My sister Katie and myself were very young children when this horrible deception began. I was eight and just a year and a half older than she. We were very mischievous children and we wanted to terrify our dear mother, who was a very good woman and very easily frightened." '—Joe Nickell, 'A Skeleton's Tale: The Origins of Modern Spiritualism,' *Skeptical Inquirer* 32(4) (July–August 2008). [Available at: www.csicop.org/si/show/skeletons_tale_the_origins_of_modern_spiritualism]

PAGE 64, *Eglinton-shaheb*: William Eglinton (1857–1933). 'Particular interest attaches to that phase of his mediumship known as Psychography, or slate-writing. [. . . C]ommon school slates were used (the sitter being at liberty to bring his own slates), and after being washed, a crumb of slate pencil was placed on the upper surface and the slate placed under the leaf of the table, pressed against it and held by the hand of the medium, whose thumb was visible on the upper surface of the table. Presently the sound of writing was heard, and on the signal of three taps being given, the slate was examined and found to contain a written message. In the same way two slates of the same size were used, bound tightly together with cord, and also what are known as box slates, to which a lock and key are attached. On many occasions writing was obtained on a single slate resting on the upper surface of the table, with the pencil between it and the table.'—Arthur Conan Doyle, *The History of Spiritualism*, Vol. 2 (1926). [Available at: gutenberg.net.au/ebooks03/ 0301061.txt]

'Of all the famous mediums in America and Europe of those days, Mr. Eglinton was supposed to be the best and the most reliable. He acquired a worldwide reputation as a psychical and materialising medium. At the instance of a few keen spiritualists of Calcutta, he came to our city in the middle of November, 1881. [. . .] While in Calcutta, Mr. Eglinton gave demonstrations of his wonderful super-normal powers in the houses of some European and Indian gentlemen. [. . . Of these,] the following are worth mentioning: Spirit writing on slate, on white paper and blank card, materialisation of spirits, levitation (i.e. floating in air), apport (i.e. passing through solid substance), and conveying of letters between London and Calcutta in a moment.'—Mrinal Kanti Ghosh, 'W. Eglinton, the Famous Medium' in *Life Beyond Death*

(New Delhi: Cosmo Publications, 1999), pp. 143–56; here, pp. 143–4.

PAGE 65, *William Stead's Borderland magazine . . . Miss Julia's spirit*: William Thomas Stead (1849–1912), British journalist, editor and publisher who founded the periodical *Review of Reviews* (1890). After becoming increasingly interested in spiritualism, he founded the spiritualist quarterly *Borderland* in 1893. Stead claimed to be in receipt of messages from the spirit world and, in 1892, to be able to produce automatic writing. His spirit contact was alleged to be the departed Julia A. Ames, an American temperance reformer and journalist whom he met in 1890 shortly before her death. In 1909, he established *Julia's Bureau*, where inquirers could obtain information about the spirit world from a group of resident mediums.

PAGE 65, *W. Stainton Moses*: William Stainton Moses (1839–1892), an English cleric and spiritualist medium. His automatic scripts began to appear in his books *Spirit Identity* (1879) and *Spirit Teachings* (1883).

PAGE 66, *Richet*: Charles Robert Richet (1850–1935). Winner of the 1913 Nobel Prize in Physiology or Medicine. Known for his investigations into the physiology of respiration and digestion, as well as epilepsy, the regulation of body heat and an array of other subjects, including parapsychology. In 1891, he founded the *Annales des sciences psychiques*. As a scientist, he was positive about a physical explanation for paranormal phenomena and coined the term ectoplasm in 1894. Author of *Thirty Years of Psychical Research* (New York: The Macmillan Company,

1923) and *Our Sixth Sense* (London: Rider, 1928), among others.

PAGE **66**, *Crookes*: Sir William Crookes (1832–1919), British chemist and physicist who worked on spectroscopy. A pioneer of vacuum tubes, he invented the Crookes Tube in 1875 and the Crookes Radiometer. Late in life, he became interested in spiritualism, conducting experiments with the famous medium Daniel Dunglas Home and attesting to the veracity of the ghost of Katie King, materialized by lady medium Miss Florence Cook.

PAGE **66**, *Meyers*: Mrinal Kanti Ghosh's *Life Beyond Death* has a mention of F. W. Meyers, so it is safe to assume that this is the same Meyers being mentioned. Frederic W. H. Myers (1843–1901) was a poet, classicist, philologist and founder of the Society for Psychical Research. He believed that a theory of consciousness must be part of a unified model of mind derived from the full range of human experience, including not only normal psychological phenomena but also a wide variety of abnormal and 'supernormal' phenomena. Author of *Phantasms of the Living* (2 volumes, 1886) and *Human Personality and Its Survival of Bodily Death* (2 volumes, 1903), among others.

PAGE **68**, *Sai Baba*: Sathya Sai Baba (Sathya Narayana Raju; 1926–2011) was an Indian guru, cult leader and philanthropist. His purported materializations—of *vibhuti* (holy ash) and small objects such as rings, necklaces and watches—along with reports of miraculous healings, resurrections, clairvoyance and bilocation, were a source of both fame and controversy. His acts were based on sleight of hand though his devotees considered them signs of his divinity.

PAGE 70, *Thakurpo*: Affectionate moniker for one's husband's brother. 'Thakur' or 'god' refers to the father-in-law; 'pola' refers to [his] 'son', shortened to 'po'.

PAGE 72, *as strong as Balaram*: The elder brother of Krishna. Etymologically, Balarama derives from the Sanskrit words 'bala' ('strength') and Rama. The stories associated with him emphasize his love of wine and his enormous strength.

PAGE 94, *Washing powder Nirma*: A brand of low-priced detergent launched in 1969, which emerged as a major, and at the time the only, competitor to Surf. Its advertising jingle, proclaiming it washed white clothes as white as milk and made coloured clothes shine and sparkle, played continually on television and before the movies in theatres, and became so popular that it still remains unchanged.

PAGE 96, *Stoneman*: 'He strikes only when Calcutta sleeps. His victims are street people, Calcutta's helpless beggars, lunatics and rickshaw pullers who share their muddy concrete beds with the city's rats, garbage and disease. And his is the perfect murder weapon in a crumbling city of broken streets—an anonymous, 50-pound concrete slab that is always taken from near his sleeping victims. He has killed seven people in the past three months, crushing their skulls with a single blow. [. . .] They call him, simply, the Stoneman. [. . .] Indeed,   the only physical evidence the Stoneman has left behind at each murder scene is the concrete slab he has used to crush his victims' skulls.'—Mark Fineman, 'A Calcutta Murderer Slinks from Depths of Depravity', *Los Angeles Times* (9 October 1989). (Available at: articles.latimes.com/1989-10-09/news/vw-166_1_murder-weapon)

PAGE 101, *Gopal Bhaar*: '[J]ester and sometimes barber to Raja Krishna-chandra of Krishnanagar in eighteenth-century Bengal. The raja, in owing allegiance both to his Hindu subjects and to the imperial Muslim nabob of Murshidabad, is continually faced with conflicts of obligation. He has the responsibility of keeping the peace, of reconciling the internal needs of the people of Krishnanagar with the external demands of the nabob. It is Gopal, the clown and trickster, who through his comic wit and playfulness inevitably enables the raja to perform this function.'— Lee Siegel, *Laughing Matters: Comic Tradition in India* (Chicago: University of Chicago Press, 1987), pp. 314–15.

PAGE 104, *Harshad Mehta*: A financier (1954–2001), the prime architect of a bank securities scam, estimated to have involved 50 billion rupees, that shook the subcontinent's banking system in 1992. Mehta was jailed in 1992. In 1995, he again caused a furore when he claimed that he made a donation of 10 million rupees to P. V. Narasimha Rao, former Indian prime minister, and the ruling Congress Party, to set him free.

PAGE 106, *Chandernagore*: Established as a French colony in 1673, when the French obtained permission to establish a trading post on the right bank of the Hooghly River. It became a permanent French settlement in 1688, and was, for a time, the main centre for European commerce in Bengal. Hence the cry of Liberty, Equality, Fraternity.

PAGE 119, *tantrick*: Deliberate misspelling of Tantric. In Bengali, tantric/tantrik also refers to godmen and/or sages engrossed in the pursuit of Tantrism.

PAGE 126, *Saha-da–Swapan case*: Satyajit Ray's cremation on 24 April 1992, was overshadowed by controversy after local goon Smashan ['Crematorium'] Swapan addressed Police Commissioner B. K. Saha as Saha-da [informally, as a brother]. The proof of proximity with the goon cost Saha his chair.

PAGE 133, CESC: Calcutta Electric Supply Corporation.

PAGE 134, *Dhanu, the LTTE's live human bomb*: Thenmozhi Rajaratnam, known as Dhanu, was a member of Black Tigers, the suicide squad of the Liberation Tigers of Tamil Eelam (LTTE), who assassinated former Indian prime minister Rajiv Gandhi at an election rally in Sriperumbudur, near Chennai, Tamil Nadu on 21 May 1991. When Dhanu bent to touch Rajiv Gandhi's feet in seeming reverence, she activated an RDX-based device (embedded with approximately 10,000 steel pellets of 2 mm each) held in a blue denim belt. At least 14 others were also killed.

PAGE 137, *loadshedding*: An intentionally engineered electrical power shutdown where electricity delivery is stopped for non-overlapping periods of time over different parts of the distribution region. Loadsheddings—which lasted upto 12 or 16 hours sometimes—were very much a part of daily life in West Bengal during the 1970s, 80s and 90s.

The two main causes of the power shortage were the inability of the West Bengal State Electricity Board, the main source of generation and supply of power in the state, to utilize its power plants to full capacity and frequent breakdowns of power plants.